Rubies & Rivals

Tale of the Stephador Clan

Gemotroplis

Companion Novella

Jack Haligo

Paperback edition, ISBN 978-0-6458634-4-4

Map by Jack Haligo
Illustrations by Kylah Davis, Jack Haligo
Cover Illustration by Jeffery E. Doherty

Printed by InHouse Publishing Pty Ltd, Australia

 A catalogue record for this book is available from the National Library of Australia

Dedicated to my dad,
for his perseverance
in helping me
publishing my works.

For greater insights into
Gemotroplis' lore, the special
plants, potions, and gemotros
subscribe to

www.gemotroplis.com

About the Author

Jack Haligo is a teenager living on the Gold Coast in Queensland, an Australian author who began writing the "Gemotroplis" pentalogy at the age of twelve years. Through his writings, Jack aims to reshape perceptions of autism, advocating for recognising the unique talents and perspectives that autistic individuals bring to society.

Jack fell in love with writing at a young age and has made it a significant part of his life. He particularly hopes his fantasy will help autistic readers shape and reflect on their thoughts and actions, guiding them to learn right from wrong and navigate the complexities of human behaviour, matters that Jack himself struggles with.

Gemotroplis reflects his vision of a fantasy world: a magical place where he could escape the harsh realities of school, bullying, and his struggles with what he describes as a 'normal life'. Autism has allowed him to see the world differently and has taught him many life lessons. In his first book, Gemotroplis (Book One) – The Stolen Heart, the main hero, Lustre, is based on Jack himself.

In this side story, Gemotroplis – Rubies & Rivals (Tale of the Stephador Clan), the hero Richard Rallian is a young man of about the same age who also shares character traits with the author.

This novella is best read before Gemotroplis (Book Two) – The Tournament.

Jack Haligo

Rubies & Rivals

Tale of the Stephador Clan

Contents

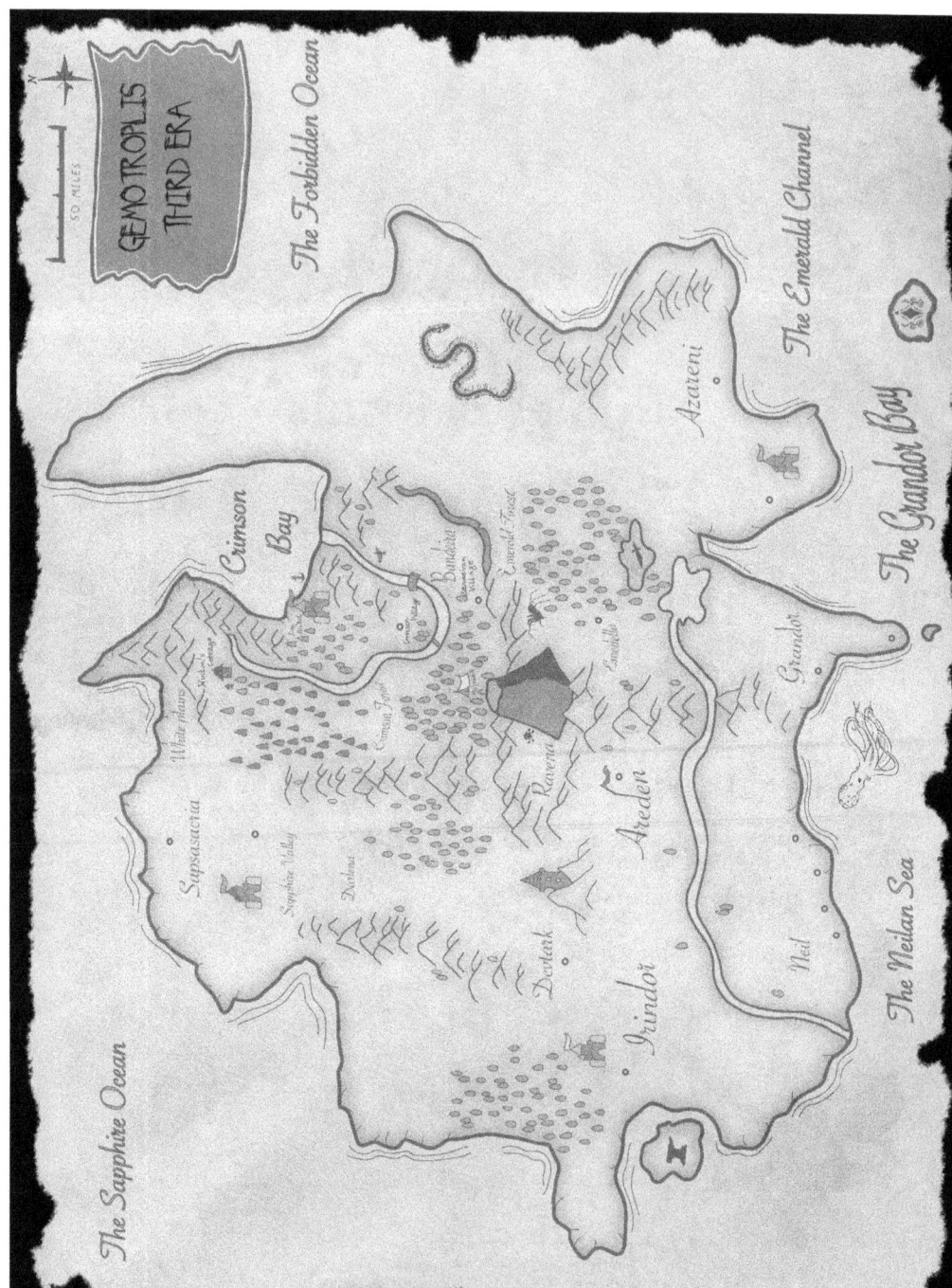

Prologue

The violence persisted in Ruby Nation, with the streets flooded with guards looking to arrest foreigners. Their actions went well beyond mere arrests, as most folks were either thrown in jail or just disappeared. The most fortunate individuals were exiled, while those with valuable skills were sent to labour camps.

During this time, a blonde-haired foreigner named Richard Rallian, a young man of only nineteen rots called the Banderian Village home. He was born a foreigner, an outsider, as both his parents were from the Topaz Nation. His father worked as a special envoy at the Ruby Palace, but his mother had not seen him for octaves. During their stay, his family had developed a deep bitterness towards the brutal reality of life in the Ruby Nation—its widespread poverty, disease-ridden streets, and the greedy emperor. So the announcement of a new war among Gemotroplis' four nations had pushed the Rallian family beyond its breaking point.

Richard's younger brother, Damian, was among the crowd of protesters gathering in the market square of Banderian Village, all holding homemade signs and demanding change. However, peaceful protests so far had proved ineffective against Emperor Maroon's decisions. Frustration soon escalated into full-blown riots, with folks overwhelmed by the oppression, waving blazing torches, and shouting at Ruby guards.

Observing from the heavens, Daradero, the cold-hearted god of death, watched as Mother Peroa, the golden-haired goddess, wept. The Heart of Gemotronia, the intact heart of their sister, a most beautiful jewel, had been unearthed, and its power had been unleashed on Gemotroplis. Peroa knew she had some explaining to do, and a confrontation with her war-hungry brother, Daradero, was now long overdue.

Now, a terrible turn was about to happen in Ruby Nation, and it was nothing short of a nightmare. Daradero smiled.

Chapter 1

The Night of the Long Spears

"**H**ey, Damian!" Richard's voice rang out, echoing through the night air, his desperate cry nearly drowned out by the voices surrounding him. The night sky hung in a deep charcoal black. Richard and his brother were adrift in a sea of protesters dressed in Topaz cloaks sewn by their mother. Pitchforks, sickles, and scythes were held high above their heads along with many blazing torches. Amidst the chaos, Richard strained to make out his brother's voice. It emerged faintly amid the uproar.

"Richard, I am over here!"

The call reached his ears, punctuated by the villagers' shouts. Richard's eyes darted upwards, searching for his brother amid the swirling chaos. On top of a mound of wooden crates, Damian stood as a solitary figure above the surging crowd like a flagpole, his silhouette etched against the haze of drifting smoke.

"There you are, I nearly lost you," said Damian with a relieved smile as Richard finally made his way to join him on top of the crates.

"Have you found mum?" Richard asked.

Damian shook his head. "No, I haven't seen mum. I'm pretty sure she is at the front, holding the sign we made." The boy's mother felt protected, as Ruby guards knew her husband was a man of influence within the Ruby Palace. From their vantage point, the brothers had a full view of the crowd below. Further down the street, a line of village guards was struggling to hold back the wave of protesters. The village guards were not equipped to handle such situations.

Soon, three large caravans hauled by paletas rolled through the town gates, each carrying dozens of guards. These weren't ordinary guards; they wielded long spears, wore heavy armour, and brandished shields known as pavises. Pavises were large oblong shields used mainly by Ruby archers. They could cover the entire body and were also particularly good at holding back protesters.

"Who are they? Father would know!" Richard was concerned.

"I reckon they're the emperor's royal guards. That means Maroon has heard our demands." Damain was quite the optimist.

The Rallian brothers hadn't seen their father in ages and had asked around the town's keep a few times. Richard's worry grew as a few guards passed around a whetstone to sharpen their swords. He was hoping they were just bluffing. "Are you sure, Damian? I don't see any emperor down here!" Richard then patted his brother on the shoulder, "Well, maybe he's sent those guards here to convey a message?"

"Umm, I hope not," Damian replied, his face now creasing with worry. All the heavily armoured guards lined up, their spears pointed inward at the crowd. They began chanting in an unforgettable tone, the words 'Hey Ho!' They intended to rush the protesters. The air grew tense as the ominous chant overpowered the protesting voices.

"What are they doing?" Damian gasped.

"I don't know," Richard replied. Soon, his brother's optimism was crushed by the line of guards lunging forward, piercing the front rows of the crowd with their spears. All the shouting and anger turned into gut-wrenching screams. It was a terrible sight.

"No!" gasped Richard, he just couldn't believe what he was seeing. Tears swelled in their eyes as the crowd scattered like a flock of startled colaies, turning the protest into a frantic stampede. It just can't be.

The royal guards lowered their spears before drawing their swords, looking for any more protesters or troublemakers foolish enough to stay put. That was the moment when the boys ran.

The royal guards were tasked not only with crushing the uprising but also with locating a woman named Glacieis, a rebellious Emerald nationer living in Banderian Village. She was well-liked and was the person who ignited the entire rebellion. Fortunately, Glacieis and her followers had been warned in advance and had managed to escape the massacre.

Soon, Banderian Village was dead silent, with a new sense of unease hanging over the streets. The dead were dragged and loaded onto wagons. That night would be remembered forever as 'The Night of the Long Spears', a night when over one hundred protesters, including Mrs Rallian, were killed by royal guards.

* * *

Half an octave later…

The two brothers stayed in the Banderian village, hiding in the family home. Richard Rallian, as the older brother, took charge. At night, they carefully searched empty houses and the remains of abandoned market stalls, looking for food or anything of value. Sometimes they found apples or preserved food in jars—food once owned by lost folk. Other villagers were doing the same to survive, but the town keep had made it clear that looting would be punished. The Banderian Jail was now overflowing.

The market square was a shambles, with only broken glass, tarnished trinkets, and rubbish among the debris.

As Richard kept scavenging, his younger brother Damian, who had been on watch, came over. "Did you see all those flyers?" Richard asked, his voice tinged with worry. "They're talking about how every man must join the army."

Damian nodded, his expression just as troubled. "Yeah, I saw them too. But, Richard, we can't join. You know what they're doing to non-Ruby folk. The guards are exiling them, and worse, some are even killed."

It was a perilous situation for the Rallian brothers, young foreigners who had lived with their parents in Banderian Village for many rotations. They had tried to blend in, adopting the customs and accent, but their origins were still obvious to guards. Their family cloaks were clearly Topaz, which they wore out of pride for their homeland. However, they would soon need to ditch such cloaks if they wanted to stay in Ruby Nation, as Emperor Maroon and his guards kept a close eye on anything not blood-red.

"I know, Damian," Richard sighed heavily. "We've got to lay low, keep our heads down. We can't risk being discovered. Emperor Maroon will loot and exploit everyone to fund his war. He won't hesitate to kill us. Life here's going to be even tougher for us."

Damian's eyes held the burden of their shared concerns. "We still don't know for sure. Stop saying war!"

Richard replied, "In any case, we must fight. I will not let mum's death be for nothing. We must become like Glacieis and her rebellion."

After his fleeting rant, Richard tossed a toy, a Topaz ferinthor, which he had just discovered in the mud. The toy was a carved gemotro, a proud symbol of Topaz resistance from the First Ruby

War, when Emperor Irindor led his Topaz cavalry to crush the Ruby Army. That day, only a few decades earlier, the ferinthor cavalry shone with fire and blinding light as the Topaz Nation defeated the evil Ruby Emperor Cranium on the fields of Ravena.

Then a sound rang out as the toy hit the shop door across the market square—a colourful chime, clear against the hollow silence. It originated from the old clock shop. The shop stood crooked and sun-bleached, with its sign barely hanging on rusted hooks, 'Tinker Clock Repair'. The windows were cracked and dust-frosted like ice. Every clock inside was thought to be broken, long since stopped, except one. That chime also marked a stroke of luck for Richard.

Richard strode over and angrily kicked in the door. The moonlight spilled into the store, showing a clock in the corner. It had its clock face open, revealing a hidden compartment. Inside, Richard saw a stylish carved box labelled 'Crimson Cigars', which was not meant to be discovered. Its vibrant crimson exterior stood out against the dull surroundings, and he carefully slid off the lid to reveal a collection of eight finely rolled cigars. The rich aroma of the cigars filled the air. These cigars were as valuable as a fine Emerald brandy or Topaz gin. They were aged cigars made from dried crimson leaves and tobacco, all flavoured and spiced before rolling—a very time-consuming process. The box also held a prized crimson oil lighter, invented by the Sapphire Nation.

He turned to his brother Damian, excitement in his eyes. "Look at this, Damian," Richard said, holding up the box of cigars. "Cigars could be worth something. It's not every day you find a box within a clock. These must be a rare find."

Damian's eyes widened as he examined the cigars. "Good find, indeed," he remarked with a nod. "Tobacco always sells well, and these might fetch us a good price. With the earnings, we could get a nice feed at Tether's Tavern." The prospect of a decent meal in these trying times was a ray of hope for the Rallian brothers, and Tether's Tavern in Crimson Village was renowned for its *'Gromblers Stew'*. They carefully stashed the box of cigars away.

It didn't take long before they uncovered their next interesting find. Looking back from the clock shop into the ruined markets offered a different perspective: hot coals and small fires were still visible at night, with some of the firelight reflecting off a metallic sign. Damian walked over. Amidst the rubble, Damian realised the spot was the remains of a blacksmith. The fallen sign read, *'Henry the IronShard Blacksmith – Fine Weapons Since Era: 2nd'*. Damian carefully sifted through the debris, uncovering remnants of finely crafted blades and weapons among the twisted metal and scattered parts. This blacksmith made exceptional weapons. Among his finds was a delicate bow with arrows, its elegance clear even in its battered state.

"Richard, look what I've found," Damian yelled, holding the bow. The IronShard Blacksmith did indeed sell top-notch weapons, and the bow was no exception. It was beautifully made; the blacksmith family was well known amongst all nations.

Richard ran over and said, "That's an excellent find, Damian. I don't think we can sell it, but you can still use it. Make sure you take good care of it." He then searched for treasure himself. After clawing through the rubble, he retrieved a magnificent longsword with a golden handle decorated with strange designs. An inscription on the blade read, *'Dazzldern another weapon by the IronShard'*. The IronShard family did indeed forge the sword. It was a recent high-valued purchase by Phil IronShard, Henry's father, from a bounty hunter named Saveth Buckleshuck. Phil only recently regained the sword because of the importance of the family legacy; it was meant to be a gift to pass down to his son, but that's a story for another time.

"Damian, you won't believe what I've found," Richard called out, his voice filled with awe. "This is a longsword and not just any longsword. It's the Dazzldern, a very famous blade. Emperor Irindor wielded this longsword during the First Ruby War." Damian's eyes widened. He was fascinated by how such a renowned sword was in the Banderian market.

"Perhaps somebody was trying to sell it. Are you sure it's not a replica? A fake?"

Richard unsheathed Dazzldern, its golden hilt shining in the light. He swung the sword a few times, feeling its weight and balance, then examined the handle.

"It's genuine, see the handle has Emperor Irindor's name carved into it. Also, the tip of the blade is chipped."

Damian smiled. "You sure know your history, don't you?"

"I guess so."

Richard was now pondering, first the Topaz ferinthor and now Dazzldern; this must be divine providence. Peroa must be guiding them to strike back.

Then his brother tested the bow. "See that bottle over there?" he said, pointing towards the rubble. In the distance stood an empty crimson cider bottle, sitting on top of some burning timber, a perfect target to test out the bow.

"Yeah?"

"I am going to hit it. Watch this!"

The bow was a stunning weapon, and the wood had remained in great condition despite its age. Damian nocked an arrow and drew the string. The bow felt perfectly balanced in his hands as he released the arrow. The missile soared through the air with precision, smashing the bottle with a loud crack.

CRACK

Shards of glass flew in every direction.

"Woah! Good shot, especially at night," Richard was impressed.

Their enthusiasm was cut short when the distant clanking of armour and the murmur of voices reached their ears. Either the bottle shattering or the clock chiming must have alerted some village guards from the keep who were approaching the marketplace. Damian and Richard exchanged worried glances and quickly secured their weapons. They would surely interpret their presence as looting, which was a death sentence, so they needed to get out of sight.

Without wasting a second, they quietly moved away. Under the cover of night, the shattered stalls and debris offered some concealment, but they needed a proper hiding spot. As they hurried through the familiar maze of laneways, they remembered an old abandoned cart behind a crumbling stone wall. They had often used this spot when playing hide and seek from their parents. They crouched behind the cart, their hearts pounding, watching the guards march past. The guards' lanterns were on full flame, clearly for high alert in search of foreigners, looters, or anything unusual. The brothers were all those things, so they knew revealing themselves was not an option.

"I am telling you, I saw Topaz cloaks," one guard said while pointing down a dark alley from which the Rallian brothers had just entered.

Richard whispered to Damian, "We can't stay here for long. If they find us, we'll be exiled or even executed on the spot."

Damian nodded in agreement, and they waited nervously for the guards to move on. The minutes felt like hours as they listened to the guards' footsteps and hushed conversations. The guards finally passed, and their voices faded into the distance.

"We have to be more careful," Damian said softly. "Let's get back home and lock the door. We can't risk being caught like this again. The Banderian Jail is full."

Richard agreed, and they headed back to their family home, this time far more cautious. Their hands shaking from the close call, they locked the door and put away their weapons.

"In the morning, we can head to the Crimson Village and sell these cigars," Richard said. The boys knew they had a long journey ahead of them. So, at dawn, amidst the morning haze, the two young lads disguised themselves and headed out of Banderian Village. They had turned their topaz cloaks inside out, revealing a brown, earthy colour, and made wigs to hide their faces. Richard devised this plan to avoid being recognised. Even though the wigs weren't very convincing, it was enough to get by.

Richard leaned in close to Damian, his voice hushed and urgent. "Remember, if you see any guards, don't panic, just act normal. Pretend you are an old woman or something." Damian tugged at his brother's cloak nervously. "Okay, Richard."

They pushed on through the gate, leaving Banderian Village

behind and heading on foot into the sprawling wilderness. Damian sighed deeply, casting a worried glance at the road ahead. "This is going to be quite the walk, isn't it?" Richard nodded.

"Yep… The Crimson Village is about three days away on foot."

As the sun rose on the horizon, the boys stopped to build a campfire. They had only travelled a few miles from Banderian Village into the vast farmlands, but the cold wind had slowed them down. The farmlands were golden wheat fields that turned into grassy plains once harvested. The brothers were freezing and hungry. "Wait here, Richard. I am going to find us some food." He pointed to a large fallen tree by the side of the road, which the strong winds had blown over.

Damian readied his bow and disappeared, while Richard used the Sapphire lighter for the first time. He rolled his thumb on the small flint wheel, and flame ignited, so he lit a pile of twigs and grass found beneath the tree trunk. He then huddled beside the tree for protection from the wind. Not a soul was in sight; the road had no travellers. The winds were too strong that day.

The flickering flames offered little warmth. The wind was cold against his skin, and he wrapped his cloak around himself. Richard looked up at the sky, feeling some faint warmth from the sun.

"Thank you, Peroa, for this disguise and this wig. I would freeze without it," chuckled Richard. Before long, Damian came back from hunting. He held two peculiar gemotros, yellow rat-like creatures with sharp teeth and beady eyes. They were reatrits, not a delicacy but a source of sustenance. Damian held up the two reatrits proudly, with the arrows still protruding. "Well, I didn't find a feast. At least we will have breakfast." Damian then proudly added, "Caught them clean through, with my new bow."

Richard examined the catch. "They don't look very appetising, but we can't be picky out here. Let's slow-cook them over the campfire." It was better than starving. Using their daggers, they skinned off the odious fur, removed the entrails, and skewered them on sticks, setting them over the smoking campfire to roast. The smell of the meat cooking filled the air, serving as a welcome distraction from the wind that blew smoke into their eyes.

Damian glanced at the food. "I've never eaten reatrit before, I wonder what they taste like?"

"Well, just a heads-up. I've heard they taste as bad as they look."

As the meal slowly cooked, they huddled by the campfire late into the day, their spirits lifted by the idea of a warm meal; the two boys hadn't had a hot meal since their mother was murdered; she always cooked and provided for them. After the two boys finished eating, they huddled together and drifted into a restless sleep. "Goodnight, Richard," Damian said, even though the afternoon sun was still high in the sky. The tree was sheltering them from the wind.

"Goodnight."

They slept into the night, well fed, just a few miles from home. Amidst the night, Richard dreamt of a time when he was just a toddler, sitting on his mother's lap. She cradled him in her warm embrace and told him a story. His mother's voice was soft and soothing as she spoke, *'The Stephadors, my sweet, are gemotros of incredible grace and beauty. They are born from fire, and they die from fire. Some people think they are furious monsters, but I know they are not. They are just misunderstood creatures with striped fur made from flame. The manes' flames are the colour of the purest* topaz.'

Richard's young eyes sparkled with wonder as he listened to every word. His mother whispered tenderly, *'They were protectors of Topaz Nation, guardians of its people, and symbols of hope and freedom. They always watch over us, ensuring our safety.'*

'*One day, I wish to meet one myself!*' young Richard said.

But then, Richard saw his mum being dragged away from him. He heard her scream, watching her body fade into the darkness. He felt so empty, so lost.

Now only half awake, "Mum!" he cried. The darkness grew deeper, swallowing his dream. "Please…Don't leave me!"

The tale of the stephador stayed in his mind; he bore the emotional weight of his mother's story. This dream would shape his future actions. A strong gust of wind sent sparks flying from the campfire, startling Richard completely awake. He sat up, drenched in a cold sweat, his breath shallow and uneven. "Damian, wake up."

Damian sat up as well, concern clear on his face. "What's wrong? Was it a nightmare?"

Richard trembled, his voice shaky. "Yeah, it was about mum. I miss her so much!"

Sitting closer to the campfire, they took comfort in each other. "It's okay, Richard," Damian said, trying to help his older brother.

Richard decided to open the crimson cigar box. He never thought he would want to smoke. Nervously, he chose one of the eight cigars inside the box and lit it with a piece of wood from the fire. He took a long, contemplative drag. The warm, earthy aroma enveloped him, and he felt a moment of peace.

"This cigar… It helps. I feel heaps better now."

Damian, watching Richard with a bemused expression, finally spoke up. "I thought you were planning to sell those cigars?"

Richard took another drag, exhaling a puff of smoke before replying. "Well, Damian, I've had a change of heart. I might need them…"

Damian knew his brother's mental state was much more important than smoking. "Fair enough. But what's the plan if we're not selling the cigars?"

Richard leaned back into the grass. "We'll find something else to sell, Damian. We need to keep our eyes open."

Soon, the campsite was bathed in morning light, and the relentless wind had fallen silent. The campfire was now just a pile of smouldering embers. Richard repacked his treasured cigars, and the brothers pressed on their journey towards Crimson Village.

Chapter 2

Stephadors Pounce

The Rallian brothers kept walking. They passed many travellers on the road, mostly men walking in the opposite direction. In response to the flyer, a steady flow of men still made their way towards the Ruby Army camp in Bandeira. Being in disguise, no one stopped the boys; they also thought it best to step off the road whenever they saw any Ruby guards. The boys' youth allowed them to cover many miles quickly. Late in the afternoon, they spotted an old, dilapidated windmill standing in the middle of a wheat field that hadn't been harvested. Its blades lay scattered on the ground, and its structure had collapsed, a shadow of what it once was. It appeared to have fallen only recently. Damian gestured toward the windmill and raised an eyebrow.

"Do you reckon there's anything valuable in there? Let's check it out!" The brothers dashed across the wheat field until they reached the other side. Richard carefully inspected the windmill and shook his head.

"No, Damian. You will only find reatrits in that old pile. There would be nothing of value here." With that, they continued their journey, leaving the old windmill behind.

The sun hung low on the horizon, casting a final golden hue

over the vast expanse of farmland. Richard and Damian had been walking for hours and were exhausted. They planned to rest, as Crimson Village was at least another day away. Then their eyes widened at the sight unfolding before them. Something was in the distance—a heavily armoured caravan slowly approaching from the south. Two pelatas, giant centipede-like gemotros, pulled the caravan. A few guards armed with crossbows clung to its sides, escorting it.

The sun's dying rays reflected off the iron walls of the carriage. It wasn't like a normal merchant caravan; it had spikes along the bottom to stop people climbing up, and armoured plates nailed to every exposed surface. Richard was filled with awe.

"Look at that, Damian." His brother squinted to get a better look. "I've heard stories about these caravans, but never seen one. They're transferring rubies from the mines to the palace, right?"

Richard nodded. "Yeah, there must be hundreds of them in there." The temptation to get closer and the thought of the riches within were irresistible. "Quickly, there are guards; we must hide!" Richard warned. They hurriedly moved off the road into a hidden spot amongst tall, swaying grass, where they could watch the caravan unnoticed. It was getting dark. Their eyes tracked the caravan as it slowly drifted past them. But as they hid in the grass, the fascination with what lay inside that caravan remained strong. They knew they'd be taking a huge risk if they dared to grab this chance. Their craving for wealth conflicted with their fear of getting caught, and they faced a monumental decision.

"So... what should we do?" Damian whispered. Richard fell silent for a moment.

"Umm... I reckon we should do this!"

"Do what?" Damian replied.

"Let's rob this caravan."

Damian's eyes darted to his brother, then quickly back to the caravan. "Are you mad? We'll be killed!" But Richard's gaze stayed fixed on the caravan.

"We have to try, remember what the Ruby guards have done to mum and everyone else. We have to fight back." Damian fell silent. His brother's words struck a chord. He thought of their parents, the life they once knew, and the future they might have if they could get their hands on some of those rubies.

"Okay..." He agreed. "Let's do this!"

The brothers began their move. They crept silently through the tall grass, keeping low and out of sight. The wind and rustling grass helped hide their approach. When they got close enough to the caravan, the brothers nodded to each other, their hearts pounding in their chests. This was their one chance. In one swift jump, they pounced from their hiding spot, their cloaks and wigs transforming them into highwaymen. Richard unsheathed his longsword, Dazzldern, and leapt onto the road, blocking the caravan's path. Damian emerged from the other side, his bow drawn and arrow nocked, shouting and waving his arms frantically.

"Stop! Stop the caravan!" Richard's voice rang out.

The guards were elderly men, too old for frontline battle. Their only job before retirement was to guard Royal Treasury caravans, but now they were taken entirely by surprise. They exchanged bewildered glances, momentarily frozen. The coachmen at the front tugged the reins, bringing the caravan to a sudden stop. The two pelatas hissed in discomfort, their many legs twitching.

"Well, well, well," Richard said, trying to sound braver than he felt. "Looks like we have a bit of a situation here. I'm Richard Rallian, Leader of the Stephador Clan." At first, all the guards seemed spooked, but once they saw the threat, they did nothing but scoff. Two kids trying to rob them, announcing their identity and wearing wigs, seemed utterly ridiculous. "Oi - get out of the way before we shoot you!" a guard shouted, his voice tinged with amusement.

"Yeah! Go back to your mummy!" One coachman again teased, holding out a lit lantern.

But then Richard snapped. In a sudden rage, he performed a Topaz spell, making the required circular motion with his arm, a magic taught to him by his father. He then released the incantation.

"Loomapa-lingera!"

A striking yellow light filled the air. The light flickered around him briefly before converging on its target through his aimed palm. In a flash, an unfortunate coachman was turned to stone, his face frozen in a perpetual gasp of fear. The lantern struck the ground.

"Nobody else has to get hurt!" Richard added. The remaining two old guards were shocked, their scepticism replaced with terror.

"By Peroa, they're Topaz! He will turn us all to stone!" Realising they were facing a real threat, the guards complied. Damian kept his bow trained on the guards.

"Toss your weapons over the side, nice and slow," he called out. The guards exchanged uncertain glances. One of them, clearly the leader, raised his hands in surrender.

"Easy now, boys. Let's not do anything rash."

Richard took a step forward, Dazzldern glinting in the fading light. "I'm not feeling particularly patient. Weapons now!" With a curse, the guards tossed their crossbows and swords over the side of the caravan. The boys kept their weapons trained on the guards as they disarmed.

"Now, get down from there," Richard called out. The guards exchanged glances and climbed down from the caravan. Damian kept them at arrow point, their hearts pounding in their chests. The caravan pelatas were well trained for such circumstances; they stood there waiting for the coachman's orders. Richard turned to the remaining coachmen as the second guard hit the ground. "And you lot, get down from there!"

The coachmen, each a grizzled-haired bloke, climbed down from their perch. Richard and Damian kept their weapons trained on the group, their minds racing.

"Well, this is not good," Richard said, trying to sound calm.

Damian kept his bow fixed on the group of four. "Shut up and keep moving," he called out. The guards and coachmen exchanged glances and started walking steadily down the road. The brothers' hearts thumped loudly in their chests. Richard's gaze shifted to the caravan's contents as soon as the guards were a safe distance away. "Well, here goes nothing," he said, sheathing his sword.

Damian kept his bow trained on the guards. "Hurry it up, Richard."

Richard nodded. He picked up the lit lantern and inspected the door, his mind racing. After a moment, he spotted a large lock holding it shut.

"Well, this is a bother," Richard said.

"What's wrong?"

"There's a lock on the door."

Damian went quiet, his mind ticking over. "Do you reckon you could open it? In this fading light?" Richard looked at the lock, his thoughts rushing. After a moment, he nodded. "I think so," he said. "But it's going to take a minute."

"Hurry it up, Richard. We have little time."

Richard nodded, then turned back to the lock. He examined it, his mind racing. After a moment, he spotted a thin piece of metal amidst the lock's mechanism.

"Ah ha," Richard said, a grin spreading across his face. After a bit of fiddling, Richard managed to dislodge the metal piece. The lock clicked open, and the door creaked as it swung ajar.

"Got it! Quickly, Damian, get this damn thing moving!"

Damian stowed his bow away and hurriedly made his way up to the coachman's seat. With a solid shove, he knocked the stone coachman to the ground using his legs. Then, with a crack of the coacher's whip, the pelatas started moving. With that, the two lads had successfully hijacked the caravan and its priceless cargo, and the old guards dared not do anything else for fear of ending up like the coachman.

"We did it! We did it!" Damian cheered from the driver's seat.

"Yeah! I know," Richard replied as he re-sheathed his sword Dazzldern. Holding the lantern, Richard peered deeper into the back of the caravan, where everything was stored. A jumble of wooden crafts and chests surrounded him. Ignoring the clutter, he went straight for the iron chest at the back, which was labelled 'Royal Rubies'. The sparkling gems that had driven them to this heist were now within arm's reach. He put the lantern down and pried open the chest to reveal a breathtaking sight…

Hours passed…

It was early morning, and the cold wind was biting into Damien's face. His eyes were fixed on the Great Ruby River. His brother was playing with handfuls of gemstones in the back. "You know, Richard, we are lucky this old bridge is still standing. I feel Banderian folk built it long ago to transport crops to Crimson Village; without it, travellers would be stuffed."

Damian's eyes were fixed on the river; he replied, "Yeah, we are lucky this bridge is still standing. I feel folk built it long ago to transport crops to Crimson Village; without it, there would be no road across the Great Ruby River to Bandeira." With that, they crossed the bridge and kept rolling towards Crimson Village. Then the pelatas unexpectedly started to gallop; the caravan was moving fast.

"Hold on," Damian yelled, resigned to letting the gemotros lead the way. Soon, the Crimson Village came into view. The caravan sped into the village, reducing their travel time considerably.

"Richard, we are here!" Damian cheered. The village was a living storybook, reflecting its vibrant past and recent struggles. The huts, built from crimson wood and stone, bore scars from recent fires. The walls were blackened, and the houses were still blanketed with ash. However, the villagers of the Crimson Village persisted. The pelatas, now only at a walking pace, passed the marketplace. Once a place of life, but now largely abandoned and fire-damaged. Some stalls were neglected, while others had been patched up; only a few villagers could be seen. The cobbled streets were quiet, except for a few voices crying out with desperation.

Come buy our goods! Come get your firewood here!

At the town square stood a grand cathedral, the heart of the village. The recent fires also damaged it. Its spires leaned precariously, and the shattered stained-glass windows revealed a sombre, abandoned interior.

"Woah! This village is not how I remember it," mentioned Damian.

Richard explained, "Do you not know? An octave ago, a fire swept through this village, burning the market and reducing everything to ashes. The cause of the fire is still unknown. That's why I knew that the cigars would sell well. The people here could smoke them to relax."

"That's terrible! Show me any village in this bloody realm that isn't burnt?" Damian pulled the reins, and the caravan stopped. He knew at least that much about driving. Out of nowhere, their hearts sank again as they witnessed another unfolding tragedy in the marketplace. A guard was wrestling a man to the ground, dust swirling around them. The cries of the man, speaking in a foreign language, were filled with anguish. His eyes were fixed on his wife and two kids, who were being torn away from him by other guards. His son wore the colours of a Topaz and was then put to the sword. The vivid, heart-wrenching scene was enough to make Damian announce, "Peroa, look at that man. He is being taken, and they're killing his family."

The struggle and chaos once again tore at their souls. "Yeah, those guards must have discovered he is foreign," Richard explained. Then Damain released the caravan reins and stood tall... His fingers trembled, but he knew what he had to do; he aimed an arrow at the enemy. Before Richard could stop him, he let the arrow loose. It soared, striking the guard through the neck. The guard then collapsed, lifeless, to the ground, a look of shock frozen on his face. The other guards appeared spooked by the sudden events and fled, abandoning the mother and daughter.

Damian stood there, bow in hand, a mixture of awe and guilt in his eyes. Silence hung heavy in the air for the next few seconds, marking a decisive moment of realisation. The world around him seemed to slow as he absorbed the gravity of what he had just done. He had taken a life... to protect another. It seemed as if the brothers had now crossed a threshold.

As the gravity of the situation settled in, villagers crowded around the caravan, a sea of anxious faces. Damian's actions had lifted the burden of fear and inspired hope.

"What's happening?" Richard questioned.

"I don't know. They think we are here to liberate them." Quickly, Richard unsheathed Dazzldern and held it above his head. In a raised voice above the murmurs, he proclaimed, "People of

Crimson Village!" Crying out to rally the crowd, his Topaz cloak fluttering in the wind, he continued, "Today we unite not against our nation, but for our nation – freedom, justice, and a brighter future. I am Richard Rallian. We've felt the weight of oppression, and I, like many of you, have seen death and experienced the pain that comes with loss. I… I am foreign. This is what makes the Ruby Nation so great: its diversity, immigrants, and foreign population. The fact that Emperor Maroon thinks he can just cast us all away is not what we stand for. I have felt the pain of loss – my parents were taken from me. I seek to avenge them! If we want to dent the emperor's plans, we must change, and it starts right now!"

The crowd cheered, inspired by Richard's words. Richard turned to his brother and whispered, "Quickly, grab the iron chest from the carriage." Damian nodded, "Okay." Then, handful by handful, the boys threw the gemstones into the crowd. The glistening rubies sparkled in the sunlight as they arced through the air, landing among the villagers. Their eyes widened in amazement and gratitude, their hands reaching to grasp them. "Here, have some more," Richard said, giving an old woman a generous handful.

"Thank you, young man, but it's food we need."

The rubies kept flowing until Richard spotted a young bloke in a crimson army cloak sneaking through the crowd. However, he didn't carry himself like a soldier. He was roughly the same age, with desperation on his face.

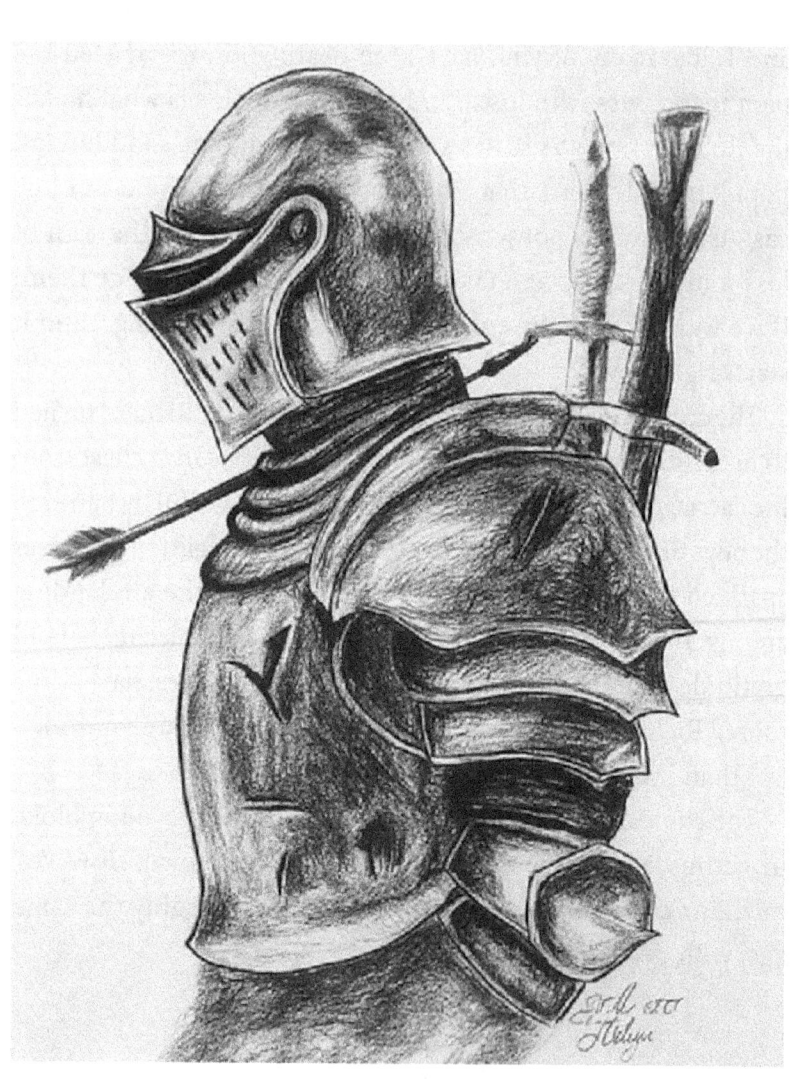

Chapter 3

A Clan's Beginning

"**H**ere you go, mate!" Richard said, giving away another handful of rubies.

"Woah!" the boy replied, as he scurried away. Bit by bit, the chests slowly emptied. Soon enough, every ruby within the caravan had been distributed among the crowd. But the joy was short-lived. Soon, the Ruby guards arrived, their stern faces and menacing armour contrasting against the joy and hope that had briefly filled the villagers.

One guard shouted in a tone that showed no defiance, "Everybody leave! Go back to your homes!" A sudden wave of fear swept through the scene. Richard, still standing with his sword lowered but his spirit unbroken, raised his voice for all to hear. "We shall not be oppressed any longer!" he declared, his words filled with unwavering resolve. However, the guards had a realisation that sent shivers down Richard's spine.

One of them pointed at the caravan and announced, "Hey, isn't that the armoured transport carriage that went missing?" His fellow guard nodded in agreement, a sense of recognition dawning. "Yeah, I think it is." Richard gasped, realising that their daring heist had been discovered. Panic set in as he cried out,

"Oh, Peroa! They're onto us!" The atmosphere was charged with uncertainty, like a thick cloud hanging over the crowd, obscuring their hopes.

Some folk were still too eager to pick up rubies from the dirt, while others, inspired by Richard's words, were ready to stand against the oppression. Some remained paralysed by fear. Before Richard could make a hasty retreat from the caravan, he hesitated. With a deep breath, he turned around and proclaimed, "Come on, everybody! Stand with us!" But despite his plea, nobody stepped forward. Equally desperate but resigned, Damian pleaded, "It's no use, Richard. They're all too scared! We have to get out of here!"

Yet, Richard couldn't shake the belief that someone in the crowd would stand up and do what was right. With each passing second, he waited and hoped. And then he waited some more. But no one stepped forward to join his rebellion. Then the guards acted. They grabbed Richard by the cloak, yanking him off the caravan. Their faces twisted in triumph as they sneered, "We've got you now. Topaz scum!" With Richard in their grip, it seemed like all hope was lost. The remaining onlookers watched in fearful silence.

But then, from the crowd, an unexpected saviour emerged. A stranger, observing the chaos from a distance, stepped forward with a heart full of anger. "Take this!" the man shouted.

SMASH

In one swift motion, the man tossed a peculiar jar filled with blue powder into the air. It shattered at the guards' feet, releasing a brilliant blue haze that engulfed the area. The guards gasped in the powdery cloud. The stranger's plan had worked perfectly. Damian and Richard held their breath.

Inhaling the strange blue dust, the guards' triumphant

expressions quickly turned to confusion. Their eyes took on a vivid, bewildering blue hue as they swayed. They staggered in disorientation, mumbling incoherent phrases and struggling to form clear sentences. It was as if they were all heavily intoxicated, lurching and grabbing at each other for support. During this drunken state, the man seized the chance. He swiftly grabbed Richard and Damian. With the two boys in tow, he hurried them to safety, navigating the winding streets of Crimson Village. Once they were out of danger, Richard Rallian couldn't contain his curiosity.

"What just happened? Who are you?" he asked, his voice desperate for answers.

"I am Derek. I have just lost my son to those guards," the man replied with a heart full of revenge. He had a small portable cauldron strapped over one shoulder and a sword sheathed by his side. The most striking detail was that he wore a Topaz robe from the Irindor School of Scholars. This official robe identified him as a foreign scholar from a renowned Gemotroplis institution. Damian was also baffled and chimed in.

"Why did you save us?"

Derek's smile widened. "Well, you saved me, my wife, and daughter from those guards just a moment ago, so I figured I'd return the favour. I used a potion known as Tipsy Tonic. When inhaled, it makes you drunker than a sailor. I brew it myself." The truth was, Derek was born in Sapphire Nation; he travelled to Irindor, the capital of Topaz Nation, to learn, and he then moved to Ruby Nation as an understudy to the Crimson Chalice. He hoped to discover the master brewer's many secrets.

Richard looked at Derek, impressed. "Wow! That's pretty cool," Richard remarked. Swiftly, the trio fled to the outskirts of the village, where they could no longer hear the sounds of guards marching.

However, their safety was short-lived, as two Ruby guards were hiding among the underbrush.

One sprang forth with deadly intent. Within seconds, he released an arrow that found its mark. Damian cried out in pain as the arrow struck his leg. The triumphant guard couldn't contain his excitement.

"Yes! I got him! Ryan, I got him!" Bear proudly announced.

Richard stared the Ruby guards in the eyes, adrenaline surging through his veins, and he didn't hesitate, raising both arms high and performing a practised dance.

"Hella-scaren-peta-shingo!" The incendiary magic ignited the surrounding plants, unleashing a spectacular firestorm that engulfed the grass and nearby shrubbery. The area erupted into chaos as flames forced the two guards to retreat.

"Quickly! Bear! Let's get out of here!" Ryan yelled, his voice tinged with urgency, as a fire twister seemed to follow them in retreat. The Ruby guards were frightened and ran; this foreigner had shown his prowess as a spellcaster. What's next, a Loomapa-lingera spell?

"I will not be burned or turned into a statue like that boy we carried to the dungeon," exclaimed Ryan. The guards quickly drank a Gone Gazz potion and teleported away.

Fortunately, the Rallian brothers weren't in the Crimson Forest, or they would have started a wildfire. Richard quickly scanned the area. His mind raced; everything was happening so fast. He soon calmed himself; no guards were around, only scorched surroundings. The spell must have frightened them off. With Damian lying on the ground in agony, Derek knelt beside him. He carefully examined the arrow in his leg, grimacing at the sight of the wound.

"I can remove the arrow, but I can't brew disinfectant. I lack the experience," Derek admitted with a heavy sigh. "Only one potion brewer in the entire Ruby Nation knows how to create an effective disinfectant, and he hasn't shared his recipes with me."

They dislodged the arrow after what felt like the longest few minutes of Damian's life. Richard then helped Derek bandage the leg with some old cloth, and they all set off towards the Crimson Forest.

"Don't worry, she'll be right!" Richard said, comforting his brother.

"Thanks, Richard." Damian smiled faintly.

"Richard, that spell you cast would have alerted the guards in the village. We need to hide in Crimson Forest so we won't be found," Derek suggested. With no choice, they headed into the forest under a full moon that night, unsure of what lay ahead.

Chapter 4

A Forest Beauty

Despite its beauty, the Crimson Forest posed some terrible dangers. Eerie sounds surrounded them, and as they walked at night, they soon heard the sudden snap of a twig in front of them. Richard drew his blade, Damian hid behind his brother, and Derek stood in fear.

Richard snapped, "Show yourself!"

As tension hung in the air, a figure stepped out from the foliage. Her blonde hair, identical in colour to Richard's, caught the dappled moonlight. The newcomer, a beautiful young woman of only twenty rots, radiated the goddess-like beauty of Peroa, stepped into view, her hands now raised in a gesture of peace. "Easy there," she said, gorgeous eyes glinting with curiosity and caution. "No need for weapons. I'm not here to harm anyone."

"What's your name?" Derek asked.

The young woman revealed, "My name is Haley Tinker."

"What are you doing in this forest, all alone in the dark?" asked Richard.

"I like the nightlife, baby!" she said with an enticing twirl. She then curtsied and blew a kiss. The lads were gobsmacked; her kiss was sweeter than Ruby wine, and she was indeed sugar, spice, and all things nice. Knowing her fan base across the realm, she asked with a proud tone, "Are you lads miners? You know, I built the platform clock at the ruby mines a few rots ago."

"No!" replied Richard, disgusted by the suggestion. The Rallian family would never be miners; in his mind, that was beneath them.

"Then why are you three here? Are you hunting deer?" Haley responded with her hands on her hips. The brothers were still transfixed, lost for words, under a spell. How could a girl be so talented?

Again, Richard replied, "No."

"Well, you're not useless, are you? My dad was an inventor, a clockmaker, and a cartographer. He taught me many things before he vanished." This was a bit too much info, but the boys finally understood why she was talented.

"What d'you mean, vanished?" Derek asked.

"He closed our shop, telling me he would do something no cartographer had ever done. Then he rode his sacro selester, creating maps after my mum passed. One day, he never came back. He has taught me everything, like gears, mechanisms, leatherworking, and hunting." Richard believed her many talents were better suited to a man, so much so that he felt intimidated, which broke the spell.

"You're just too much, enough talk. Why are you here?" Richard cut in.

"I've decided to hunt grombler and maybe a deer or two, just for the fresh air," Haley said with a smile.

"Ouch. What in bloody hell!" Damain yelled in pain. His leg was throbbing with agony.

"Yes, I am here because I want to make lovely clothes from leather. I use skins to craft boots, hats, shirts, everything," she confessed with an enticing smile.

"Wait, there are no gromblers in the Crimson Forest. They only live down in Bandeira," Derek pointed out.

"Well, I am not looking for gromblers right now; I'm also looking for something else. It's my secret ingredient."

Intrigued, Richard and Derek exchanged glances, captivated by the mystery veiled behind Haley's words. "Indeed. It's a little something I add to the leather to make it softer, more colourful, and, most importantly, odourless. If you don't know, grombler leather reeks in the heat."

The group ventured deeper into the dense woods, guided only by the moonlight filtering through the towering trees. As they walked, Haley shared stories about further inventions.

"You know," Haley began with a sparkling glint in her eyes, "As much as I love working with leather, there's a different kind of magic in inventing machines. Something about making gears turn and building contraptions that move—it's exhilarating."

Richard grinned, "Machines? What contraptions are you talking about, clocks?"

Haley winked. "Ah, that's where the real secrets are. You see, I've got this secret project in mind. A contraption that could revolutionise the way we hunt gemotros. But, of course, it's all hush-hush for now. Once done, I could use it to hunt gromblers for fresh leather instead of searching for dead ones. The dead gromblers I normally come across are rotten and foul, which makes the hide unusable."

Derek raised an eyebrow, "Surely you can tell us what this secret contraption is?"

Haley laughed softly. "Well, let's just say it is nothing like folk have ever used before. It's a weapon."

Richard leaned in, curiosity evident on his face. "A weapon, what sort?"

Haley gazed over her shoulder at Richard. "I am afraid I cannot

tell you, but you can know its name, just for now! I call it...
HAVOC."

Derek chuckled, "Sounds ambitious."

Haley grinned. "Ambition is the fuel for invention. And who
knows, one day, you may see my contraption at work. But for now,
it only exists in my mind and on blueprints back at my wagon."
Derek quickly realised she seemed almost too willing to share
knowledge and secrets with strangers. She had shared so much so
quickly, knowing nothing about the brothers; this was a perilous
character trait. It's only luck that the trio had good intentions.

Beautiful and clever, but lacking judgment," thought Derek.

As they ventured deeper into the moonlit woods, the air filled
with anticipation. The golden-haired beauty walking in front of them
seductively mesmerised Richard. He was now carrying her satchel,
totally forgetting about his brother Damian, who was labouring far
behind. After a while, they reached a small clearing bathed in an
eerie blue glow. Haley pointed to a cluster of striking red flowers.

"Behold, the blood orchids. They emit this ominous blue glow,
especially in the dark, making them easy to spot. That's why I only
venture out for my secret ingredient at night."

Richard and Derek marvelled at the beauty of the blood orchids,
their blue glow casting an otherworldly ambience. "But why are
they called blood orchids?" Derek asked, his voice barely above a
whisper. Haley crouched down, gently running her fingers over
the petals.

"Legend has it, they only grow where blood has once been
spilled."

She plucked a few blossoms, then asked Richard for her satchel.
Opening it, she revealed a mixture of crushed orchid petals,
aromatic herbs, and a vial of shimmering oil.

"This, gentlemen, is my secret ingredient. Combined with

grombler leather, it makes it a beautiful red colour and softness and eliminates the stench." Richard and Derek exchanged an amazed look.

"You know, my family has been in the leather craft business for generations," her eyes reflecting the flickering light of the blood orchids. "But it wasn't until I stumbled upon the blood orchids and experimented with their properties that I truly found my calling."

"Stop, please!" said Damian after finally catching up and grabbing his leg.

"Peroa, I mean Haley, how did you come up with the idea of using these orchids in your craft?" Derek was intrigued.

Haley giggled. "It was a mix of luck and a lot of trial and error. One night, I was out in this forest, gathering mushrooms, looking for Bloodcap Widows. You know, those mushrooms are lethal and cause paralysis and death. That's when I stumbled upon a patch of these glowing wonders. I decided to sniff one and realised they smell super sweet."

Richard valued practicality. "Blood Cap Widows, now those mushrooms sound handy. I don't care for flowers." He crouched to sniff the orchids. Haley watched with a knowing smirk, expecting his reaction. As Richard inhaled deeply, hoping for a sweet scent, his face shifted from curiosity to shock and then outright disbelief. He pulled back quickly, his face twisted in confusion.

VOMIT

"These… these don't smell sweet at all! They're worse than I imagined."

Haley burst into laughter with a radiant smile, her eyes twinkling with amusement. "Oh, I tricked you. That, my friends, is why you should never believe what a stranger tells you. These flowers smell terrible. But when they are combined with grombler leather, for some reason, they completely cancel out smell."

Unbeknownst to Derek, the blood orchid served as a disinfectant when brewed. Despite having read numerous books on plants from the Royal Library, he had not come across any information on the blood orchids during his scholarly pursuits.

Derek joined in the laughter, giving Richard a pat on the back.

"Seems like this forest has a sense of humour. Beautiful flowers in appearance, but a not-so-beautiful surprise when you smell them."

Damian was trying to keep up with the group. His steps slowed, and he was breathing more heavily. The group's pace was hard for his injured leg. "Richard, could we please take a short rest?" His blood-soaked bandage was visible under the full moon as he leaned against a tree, looking tired. Richard, hearing his brother's request, turned away from Haley's beautiful appearance.

"All right then. We'll find our way out of this forest in the morning!"

A resourceful Haley suggested they build a fire to stay warm, so the group began gathering dry leaves, twigs, and branches. Damian was in too much pain to be of any help. Under bright moonlight, the other searched the forest floor for larger logs. The air was cool, and the only sounds were the hoots of the night-colaies.

As they scoured the area, Haley's keen eyes caught something unusual—a tree with red sap bleeding from the bark. She approached cautiously, inspecting the oozing liquid. Intrigued, she pulled a bottle from her satchel and began collecting the mysterious sap.

"Look at this, Richard," she called excitedly. "I reckon this might be the sap of a crimson tree. With it, I can make crimson oil."

Richard joined her, peering at the tree. "Ok. Let's take it back to the fire."

With the bottle filled, they turned to head back to the camp. Along the way, Richard spotted a weathered sign on a nearby tree. Squinting to read the faded words in the moonlight, it read 'Warning, blood, urine, and fire may attract wavires'.

Haley was dismissive of the warning, "Superstitions. I doubt they're true. I haven't seen a wavire. Let's not worry about it; we've got enough to deal with." They headed back to the campfire.

Derek was looking for a flint and steel.

"Paxta-Holla!" Haley held out her hand and cast a spell; the fire flickered with life. The immediate area was covered in light.

"Woah, that's better than a flint and steel," commented Derek. The others couldn't cast such a spell since they were all born foreign. Richard thought it was a silly spell and that it really served no purpose; he thought his Sapphire lighter was way more elegant and cool.

With the fire crackling and warmth spreading through the small clearing, Damian struggled over to be near the warmth. The group settled around him, comforting him. As Richard stared into the flames, his mind was still haunted by the nightmare from a few nights ago. 'The Night of the Long Spears' had forever scarred his memory. He tried to avoid thinking about it. He took out a crimson cigar, rolled his thumb on the lighter, and lit it.

Immediately after, he felt a little better.

"What's wrong, Richard? You seem afraid of something?" Haley was feeling emotional; her dad smoked whenever he was worried. Richard responded softly after a long drag from his cigar, "It's just nightmares, and I can't stop thinking about it. There are many unanswered questions, and I need to know more about everything!" With the firelight dancing on the crimson trees, Haley noticed Richard's thoughts lingering. Sensing an opportunity to distract him from the nightmares, she approached with a slight smile.

"Do you want to know more about this, Richard?" Haley asked, holding the bottle filled with the strange sap. Richard looked up, his eyes reflecting a fascination with her and a thirst for something more than the gloomy forest.

"What is that stuff, anyway?"

Haley settled herself next to him and began to explain. "Crimson sap. It's a nifty little trick picked up during my travels. The secret lies in the oil that can be extracted from the sap." She reached for a small pouch, retrieving an old piece of cloth, a jar filled with red berries, and a spoon. She crushed the berries between her fingers, releasing a rich, aromatic scent.

"What are those berries?" Richard asked.

"They are crimson berries, which are used to make crimson cider. Sadly, they are now rare in Ruby Nation and only grow in a few locations like here in the Crimson Forest, so it's pretty hard to get a hold of some."

"Okay then, why are you crushing them?" Richard asked another question.

"These berries are the catalyst," Haley explained. "But the real magic happens when you mix them with the crimson sap. Puncture the trunk, collect the sap, and mix it with clean water. Next, filter the mixture through a cloth to remove impurities. Stir it, apply some heat and let it simmer so that the oils can settle on top. Voilà, you've got yourself some potent crimson oil."

She encouraged him to "Give it a try. It's pretty straightforward, just filter out the gunk; we don't want any surprises when we use it."

Richard nodded. Carefully, he poured the sap through the piece of cloth and then wrung it out, filtering out all the impurities. Deep crimson liquid streamed from the bottom of the fabric into a pot, and she then stirred in water and the berries. "Now we let it simmer for a while until there is a clear layer of oil on the top!" They all watched as the oils bubbled to the top of the pot, and a layer soon formed. She took it off the heat. Once cool, she spooned off the oil into a vial.

"There you go," Haley praised him. "That's crimson oil. You're a natural brewer in the making." Richard capped the vial containing their freshly made crimson oil; he couldn't help but feel a spark of satisfaction. Even though he did very little, he felt proud of himself.

"Okay, cool. So, what does this crimson oil stuff do?" Richard asked.

"I will show you later. It's pretty dangerous," Haley said with a devious grin.

A heavy silence also seemed to cling to the air. Around the crackling campfire, the little light revealed some tense expressions on Richard, Haley, and Damian's faces. Richard had almost finished his cigar when light rain began to fall, dampening everything.

"What do you think crimson cigars are made from?" Richard broke the silence.

"Umm, I think it's tobacco blended with crimson leaves," replied Derek.

"Whatever it is, I love it," Richard chuckled.

Soon, an unknown terror was to meet the Stephador Clan; a deep guttural growl shattered the stillness. Wide-eyed and tense, the four shared anxious glances.

"T-T-That didn't sound good," stuttered Haley.

Damian, still sitting, nocked his bow and prepared an arrow.

Richard's hand fell instinctively on the hilt of his sword. The silence that followed felt deafening, the weight of the unknown pressing upon them. It was as if the night held its breath, waiting for something...

Then it happened; from the depths of the trees emerged a towering beast, a monstrous gemotro, a wavire! Its presence cast a black silhouette against the flickering firelight.

Damian shot at the beast, but to no avail; the arrow just glanced off its body.

Richard drew Dazzldern from its sheath and shouted, "EVERYBODY RUN!"

Haley quickly helped Damian to his feet, and the whole group bolted. The wavire's eyes gleamed with hunger as it looked around, searching for its meal near the fire. It didn't take long before it caught the scent of the blood of a wounded boy. It scuttled towards him, its height matching that of a man, as its eight spider-like legs pounded the forest floor. Damian was struggling to keep up; he gasped for breath. He was still too weak.

"Keep moving! Come on, Damian!" Richard's urgent command rang out through the night air. Damian panicked as he stumbled, then tripped and fell to the ground.

"No!" Haley gasped.

As the wavire fangs closed in, terror gripped everybody's hearts. Derek kept running, but Richard and Haley stopped to look.

"Damian!" Richard shouted out, fear in his eyes.

"Richard, keep going. I've got an idea!" Haley raced back to the campfire.

The wavire hovered over Damian, its legs trying to spear him to the ground. Damian rolled and rolled to avoid the attack. As Haley passed the campfire, she grabbed a flaming stick. In one daring throw, she hurled the vial of crimson oil towards the wavire, the glass shattered on impact, splattering crimson oil all over the gemotro. The wavire turned towards Haley and emitted a piercing sound. The noise echoed throughout the forest, a harrowing screech as if it knew what to expect next. Haley threw the flaming stick at the wavire.

WOOF

The stick lit the oil, burning the spider in agonising flames and lighting up the forest. Dodging the flames, Damian rolled away. The air now reeked of burning oil and the desperate screeches of the wavire.

Breathing heavily, the group watched as the wavire fled, the fiery spectacle illuminating their shocked expressions. The wavire, now defeated, ran back into the depths of the night, with fading flames retreating amongst the wet crimson trees to die.

Unbeknownst to the clan, a disgusting yellow ooze found inside a dead wavire called 'Wav-va-wire stella lo-compo' was also a secret disinfectant—an opportunity now lost in the brush. This well-guarded secret was only known to the Fletcher brothers. Jackie Fletcher, the man who had made the sign to warn travellers, would hunt the gemotro. He would then bottle the precious fluid for his brother Winston, the Crimson Chalice, who lived in the White Plains.

As the echoes of the dying gemotro faded, Richard and Haley stood amidst the flickering embers, a mix of relief and awe in their eyes. The forest was once again cloaked in damp darkness and slight rain; the fire was dying.

Derek had now returned, helping Damian back up to his feet.

"You're wondering what this stuff does? Well, it explodes. Crimson oil is the most flammable substance in all of Gemotroplis, so if you introduce a flame, it will explode with twice the power of any destructive spell known to magic."

Richard was shocked and nodded, still baffled by what he had just witnessed.

"My Peroa…" Richard stuttered. In the aftermath, they heaped plenty of fiery logs directly onto the campfire. As the rain fell, none of them was now willing to go to sleep. A few hours later, morning broke, and we were still in light rain. The group, led by Haley, trudged through the soaked forest. "I left my wagon back here somewhere." The path took them out of Crimson Forest and into an open clearing.

"Good, with a wagon, we can rest our legs," Damian announced, feeling his wound. Eventually, they all gathered around the wagon. It showed signs of wear and tear; it was falling apart. One of the wheels had broken off, lying a few feet away.

"Well, it's certainly a wagon," Richard said, attempting a bit of a joke.

"What happened here?" Derek asked. Haley sighed, her gaze fixed on the broken wheel.

"Well, that's just perfect. I need my wagon to transport my leather." Her breath fogged in the cold air as she explained further. "These dirt tracks are unforgiving and too much for my old wagon."

Despite the wear and tear, the wagon held a stash of grombler leather. A dozen thick skins were stacked, showing Haley's dedication. The sturdy and weathered leather gave off a strong smell, mixing with the scent of damp earth and rain.

"Those haven't been treated with the blood orchids yet, so they still reek," Haley said. Richard circled the wagon, looking for anything else interesting. At the front of the wagon hung a makeshift shoulder bag crafted from a repurposed wheat sack.

"Hey, Haley, what's that bag for?" Richard asked as he placed Haley's satchel into the wagon. Haley's eyes gleamed with pride as she pointed to the shoulder bag. "I made this bag to carry everything I need—flowers, tools, food, and even my blueprints and sketches. I have a satchel for all my ingredients and a shoulder bag for everything else."

"It's impressive, Haley. You're good at everything! Leatherwork, weaving, inventing, hunting," remarked Derek with genuine admiration in his voice. "Thanks," she replied and blew him a kiss.

"R-Richard. It's so cold," Damian coughed. Richard had again forgotten his brother among Haley's radiance. "Okay, we can find some shelter."

"Why don't we all just sit under my wagon until the rain passes?" Haley suggested.

"Good idea!" Derek was the first to dive under, escaping the rain. They all huddled under the wagon, using it as a roof, finding a moment of peace amidst the now heavy rain.

As the rain drummed on the wagon above them, they kept spirits high by chatting away. Haley swiftly grabbed her shoulder bag from above and tucked it under the wagon to keep it dry; she was worried about her blueprints.

"So, is anyone hungry? I've got some leftover crimson berries in my bag."

"Yes!" Derek and Richard shouted immediately; however, Damian said nothing. He was shivering with chattering teeth.

"Hey Damian, do you want some?" Haley offered.

"No thanks, but a blanket would be nice." His voice was very weak. They all devoured the leftover crimson berries, which, although quite sour, nourished their collective hunger.

"So, what else do you have in that shoulder bag?" Derek asked, filled with curiosity. Haley smiled, "Well, you guys haven't seen my secret invention yet. I could show you if you don't tell anybody." She carefully pulled out a set of scrolls tied with a ribbon. The paper was slightly wrinkled from the cold, but the intricate drawings were still visible.

"Behold, my invention!" Haley exclaimed, unravelling blueprints for everyone to see. Derek's eyes widened with excitement; he was most interested. "It looks like a crossbow?"

"Exactly!" Haley nodded. "I've been working on this for weeks. Imagine the possibilities, especially when we're out here facing the challenges of the wild!" Richard leaned in for a closer look.

"What does it do?"

Haley pointed to the mechanical part of the crossbow. "You see, it's not like any normal crossbow. It's Haley's Automatic V-String Obliterating Crossbow, or... HAVOC. It fires up to 210 bolts a minute. That's about three and a half arrows every second!" Haley said enthusiastically.

"Wait... How can it fire half an arrow?" Richard questioned.

Derek let out a disappointed sigh. "Didn't you go to school, Richard?"

"What is... school?"

They all shared a good laugh, chatting until the rain finally eased off. Afterwards, Haley got to work reattaching the wheel, while Richard and Derek took the chance to survey their surroundings.

"Damian, how are you holding up?" Richard inquired.

Damian was a pillar of strength throughout the morning's walk; he now leaned against the wheel, fatigue etched across his features. His breathing was in measured puffs, and beads of sweat trickled down his forehead. "Just a bit tired," he reassured his brother.

With the other wheel fixed, Haley stood up, brushing her hands off. "We're all sorted. Let's get moving."

Determined to press on, Richard and Derek began to tow the wagon using the harness. "Let's get going to the Ruby Palace," said Richard with vengeance on his mind. Damian was now lying flat on the grombler leather, far too weak to walk. The clan had to cross miles of hilly terrain to reach the palace. Damian's laboured breathing became increasingly apparent as they pulled the wagon along a dirt track through the undulating landscape.

The clan pressed on; the wagon creaking with each strained

pull. The foothills' terrain was rugged and unforgiving until older Derek couldn't take it anymore.

"Can we please stop for a bit?" Derek asked between breaths.

"No, we have to keep going," Haley said as she took Derek's spot, pulling the wagon.

The group had ventured deep into the heights of the foothills, away from the trading roads, along pathways that were not fit for wagons. The Ruby Place was still many hours away. Lying in the back of the wagon, Damian sighted the treetops of Crimson Forest. A great mountain range bordered the forest on the western horizon. The Great Ruby River dominated the landscape, starting far in the northern mountains, splitting the vast forest in two as it carved its way past the border mountains. The river provided a true contrast of colour against the rocky outcroppings and down onto the grassy plains, giving life to the Ruby Nation. A distant glimpse of smoke from Crimson Village could be seen to the south. The scenery gave Damian some peace as he felt his body giving in.

Soon, the whisper of the wind was filled with the echoing calls of distant colaies, both whistling down from the craggy peaks and now treacherous inclines. Damian's heart had slowed, and fatigue had overwhelmed him; he had succumbed to his wounded leg.

"Come on, stay awake!" Richard called out from the front of the wagon. Usually, Damian would reply with a few reassuring words from the back of a slow-moving wagon, but instead, he let out a deathly moan.

"Damian!" Richard's voice shook with fear as he rushed to his brother. The others in the group halted, and all gathered around Damian, their faces etched with concern.

"What's wrong?" Richard asked with urgency. Damian coughed violently before pointing down at his leg. Derek quickly examined the injury by unwrapping the bloody bandage. He was then immensely concerned. "He's got a badly infected wound," he announced, his voice heavy with sorrow. "It must have been from that arrow in the Crimson Village."

Haley tried to comfort Damian, her eyes filled with worry and helplessness. "We need to do something, anything!" Damian contorted on the back of the wagon. He gripped Richard's hand tightly, their fingers entwined, and his voice came out as a strained gasp. "I'm... sorry," he wheezed. "I tried, but I can't keep going."

"Quick! Do we have any Muzzle Mud?" Richard cried out. Unknown to Richard, the potion did not cure an infection.

They didn't!

Richard's tears fell to the ground, mingling with the dust of the unforgiving terrain. He held Damian close, whispering words of reassurance, urging him to stay awake. But Damian's breath grew shallow; then, a seizure took hold. His grip on Richard's hand tightened dramatically, then suddenly weakened.

His eyes, once vibrant and full of life, now dimmed. In his final moments, he gave a weak smile and a final farewell.

"It's okay, Richard," Damian said, taking his last breath. "At least I can see mum again. Peroa will permit it!"

Richard, choked with grief, kept holding Damian's hand as he slipped away. The world around them seemed to fade. Time felt frozen, and Richard wept openly as he cradled his brother.

All stood in sombre silence, their hearts heavy with the weight of their loss. Derek, the closest they had to a doctor, closed Damian's unseeing eyes, a final act of tenderness and respect. Haley placed a comforting hand on Richard's shoulder. "He's at peace now, Richard. He is with Peroa!"

Richard, his grief profound, nodded silently. With trembling hands, he retrieved a cigar from his pocket and lit it using the Sapphire lighter. As the aromatic smoke enveloped him, he seemed transformed. His tears dried, and his expression shifted from one of sorrow to one of action.

He looked at Haley through a haze of smoke and spoke with a voice of newfound strength. "We need to bury Damian properly!"

Together, the group dug a shallow grave in the rocky ground of the foothills, their hands working in unison. It was a tribute to a fallen mate and brother whose journey had ended far too early. Richard placed Damian's bow and quiver in the grave, a token of remembrance, before they filled it with rocks and dirt. However, they kept his topaz cloak, which Richard then passed on to Haley to wear. "You are now part of the Stephador Clan. Wear this to remember my brother!"

The three then stood in respectful silence for about an hour, all gathered around Damian's grave. Richard's heart filled with anger.

Chapter 5

Richard's Wine

Many hours passed before the track widened to meet a busier trading road. It was odd; neither a peasant nor a Ruby guard was seen. That was a relief, as Richard was angry, and his desire for revenge was clear. A confrontation was likely. He never spoke to Derek or Haley. They all decided it was better to stay silent. The clan continued hauling the wagon in a sombre mood.

After a day's travel across lush green knolls, the road led to a small cliff. They could see the northern edge of the Crimson Forest hugging Crimson Bay, a blend of deep sea blue and the forest's red hue. The Ruby Palace stood prominently, looking imposing and grand in the distance. Royal Ruby Town stretched out beneath the palace like a servant before a king.

The air was thick with anticipation as they carefully guided the wagon down the dirt track; the expected joyous welcoming of Royal Ruby Town calling them forward. As they pulled the wagon along the winding road, descending the cliff, the first droplets of rain began to fall again, a gentle prelude to the coming shower.

"Raining again?" Derek said as his first words that day.

The group's walking pace appeared to pick up, now in rhythm with the patter of raindrops on the hard road.

Reaching the outskirts of Ruby Town, the rain intensified, casting a melancholic gloom over the dilapidated buildings. The marketplace was deserted, apart from a few forest deer that had made themselves at home in the square. The entire town looked dull. Rundown structures seemed to blend with the grey of the rain-drenched sky, creating a scene of bleakness. The deer were a sign that people were in hiding, as they would usually be frightened.

"Where is everyone?" Haley asked.

Most are in bed, too knackered to move, starving! The nation is without a crumb of food; thank Peroa for pickled sardines. Only the emperor feasts now after this declaration of war," Derek replied ominously.

"It's like the village is mourning," Richard remarked, his voice hushed as they pulled the wagon through the sombre streets. Haley nodded in agreement and said, "Maroon's statue is casting a long shadow over this place."

They left the village without hesitation, heading further west and approaching the northern edge of the Crimson Forest; the rain showed no sign of easing. The trio's clothes were soaked through, and they desperately needed a campfire. Richard spotted a spot where the tall trees formed a dense canopy, providing a natural shelter. The site was ideal for camping and lighting a fire. Soon, the clan was warming up, but the rain turned to snow as a cold snap set in. Richard's sharp eyes then caught a flickering light among the trees. Two figures under a half-finished shelter with a fire were asleep in the distance. They looked like guards. Their armour was soaked, and snow was starting to gather on their helmets.

"Guards," Richard whispered, his hand instinctively gripping the hilt of his sword. "Over there!" Richard's eyes narrowed as the snow continued to flutter down. He recognised these guards. He stood up, fuelled by a surge of anger. These were the same guards who had shot Damian—the very arrow that had led Damian to infection and death.

"The ones who shot Damian." Richard's voice was low but full of intensity. The memory of Damian's pain, the agony on his face, pushed Richard forward without hesitation. "We can't let them go…" Richard declared, his grip on his sword tightening.

Then, he drew Dazzldern and began approaching the two guards. Haley and Derek exchanged worried glances. "Wait, Richard. What are you doing? You can't just walk straight up to them like some sort of hero." Before Haley could finish, Richard pushed past her, showing no concern for what she had to say.

Nothing could stop Richard now.

The air was filled with white snowflakes as Richard silently moved towards the two guards, like a stephador sneaking up on its prey and ready to strike. Dazzldern, his longsword, shimmered menacingly in the faint moonlight. The guards, oblivious to him, were snoring beneath their makeshift shelter, constructed from leaves, sticks, and soaked wood. Richard's imposing figure emerged from the white haze, holding Dazzldern, an unexpected attack.

Without hesitation, Richard lunged at them, sword arcing through the air. Instantly, one of the guards awoke and drew his sword. The clash of steel echoed through the forest. Ironically, the guard was caught off guard by the sudden assault. He struggled to parry Richard's relentless onslaught.

"You! How did you find us?" yelled Ryan.

Amidst the dance of swords, Richard pressed home the attack, his voice cutting through the storm sharper than his blade. "Who shot Damian?" he demanded, each word laced with a fierce intensity that mirrored the now-snowstorm's fury.

The other guard was now also awake, but his blade was frozen and stuck in its sheath. Ryan, the guard, panicked. Fear was marked across his face. He stammered a response, pointing trembling fingers towards his mate. "It was him! It was Bear! He shot the arrow!" His voice quivered with fear, knowing he was no match. He surrendered, dropping his blade in the snow.

Richard's eyes, blazing with a storm of emotions, were now fixed on the accused guard. "Are you right-handed or left-handed?" he roared.

Bear then hesitated, "Why does it matter?"

Richard repeated the question, this time even louder, "Tell me! Are you right-handed or left-handed?"

"L-L-Left-handed," Bear admitted.

Fuelled by rage, Richard seized the left-handed guard and dragged him deeper into the forest. Ryan was left alone, paralysed with fear. Richard's grip on Bear was unyielding. He took Bear to a spot far from anybody's view. He glared into the guard's eyes in the dim light as he forced Bear to place his left hand on a boulder. Then in one swift, merciless stroke.

CHOP

Richard severed the guard's bow fingers. Bear writhed in pain as he saw his two fingers hit the snow. His cries were carried away by the wind into the abyss of the storm.

"That will teach you," Richard said. Then, just like that, he turned away, leaving the guard moaning on the forest floor.

Soaked to the bone, Richard trudged out of the woods, his steps heavy with the weight of the load. His heart had finally found some relief from the ache. Haley and Derek, waiting for Richard, looked worried and curious. As he drew near, Derek asked, "Richard, what happened back there?"

Richard's eyes were ablaze. He met Derek's gaze and, in a sombre voice, he replied, "I did it for Damian." Haley, eyes widening with shock and sympathy, hesitated before asking, "What did you do?"

Richard nodded, his gaze fixed on the distant mountains. "I took care of it. Made sure his shooting days were over. You can't draw back the bowstring if you don't have any fingers now, can you?"

Derek, sensing the storm within Richard's soul, approached cautiously and reassured, "I understand your pain, but revenge won't bring Damian back. We need to focus on what lies ahead and honour his memory in a way that would make him proud."

Richard's jaw tightened, fists clenched under his snow-soaked topaz cloak. Eventually, he nodded in reluctant agreement. "Nobody talks to me until I have lit a crimson cigar." Haley, out of nowhere, whispered an ominous quote:

"For each raindrop, a tear has once fallen," she reminded him, "Remember, you are not the only one who has lost a brother, Richard. You are not the only one with pain!"

Richard stopped and stared at Haley. "How do I know that? How do I know there are people out there who are suffering a loss this bad, just like me?" Richard snapped.

Haley's response was both calm and collected: "Just look up, Richard."

Richard gazed at the cloudy night sky, snow battering his face. "I guess…"

Derek, Haley, and Richard sat in a circle around a crackling campfire, its warm glow flickering on their faces—quietly reflecting on what had just happened. The atmosphere was now fairly calm. Haley finally broke the silence, her voice gentle in the peaceful night. "Richard, how are you holding up?"

Looking into the dancing flames, Richard initially offered a simple, "Fine."

Haley's eyes, full of empathy, locked onto him as she leaned in. "My mum always told me that if someone says they're fine, they're usually not."

Richard's expression shifted as if he had suddenly remembered something he'd buried deep inside his mind. In response, he reached into his pocket, pulled out a cigar, and lit it with the flames of the campfire. It had to be a memory, but whatever it was, he quickly drowned it with a deep drag from his crimson cigar. Curious and persistent, Haley gently asked, "What's bothering you, Richard?"

She continued, "You know, my mum also used to say that if someone answers with a *nothing* when asked a question, they don't mean…" For a moment, Richard hesitated, his eyes fixed on the ember-lit tip of his cigar.

"Nothing," he finally muttered.

Not willing to give up easily, Haley leaned in even closer now, wrapping her arm around him. He pushed her arm away. His voice was now laced with authority, "Stop talking, leave me alone!"

Then again, more awkward silence settled over the group. After a few minutes, Derek, who had been quietly watching the exchange, decided to speak up and steer the chat elsewhere. He asked Richard, "Why do you even smoke those things?"

With a weary sigh, Richard took a long drag from his cigar before replying, "It…helps me forget… bad memories." The smoke spiralled into the night air as if carrying away some of the weight burdening Richard's soul.

Derek sighed. "If it's Damian, I'm sorry. I don't know how to brew disinfectant."

"It is NOT DAMIAN!" Richard boomed in a sudden rage. Everything fell silent again, and nobody said another word until morning came.

* * *

While everyone was still asleep, he sought a plan to infiltrate the palace. He turned his cloak inside out and headed back to Ruby Town. Richard strolled through the narrow, rain-soaked alleys, where the faint glow of lanterns still cast an eerie ambience on the weathered buildings. He was pondering the name of his clan. Richard believed the stephador was the perfect choice, a gemotro often mentioned in his mother's stories and symbolised the flame in his heart. The creatures hunted in small packs, just like his clan. The gemotro symbolised the imperial Topaz Empire and an untamed force of Peroa. Visually, a stephador looked like a massive tiger with fur of magic flame. The gemotro was most feared amongst Topaz lore; it could also breathe magical fire; however, his mother always painted the gemotro in a kind light.

The air was thick with the smell of earth, and the rhythmic pounding of raindrops echoed as Richard searched for a way to sneak into the palace. His steps led him to a discreet building tucked away at the edge of the market square. A faded sign with the words 'Royal Library' etched upon it. The Royal Library was visited by folks who enjoyed books, but for some reason, Richard was there. The door creaked open, and Richard stepped into a realm of musty air and dusty books.

Rows of weathered books lined the shelves. Richard wandered through the aisles, scanning the titles. As his fingers traced the spines, he stumbled upon a book that beckoned him. The title 'The Ruby Palace' was in faded gold letters on a frayed leather cover. Richard pulled it from the shelf and skimmed through the pages. Strangely, the book was without an author. It felt ancient in his hands, its pages yellowed with age. The pages unfolded a tale written by an unknown hand, revealing the secrets woven into the very foundations of the

Ruby Palace. Intricate illustrations accompanied the text, depicting something Richard couldn't fathom. A secret passage lay beneath the palace. Richard's eyes widened as the realisation dawned.

Armed with new knowledge, Richard approached the librarian's desk. An older woman, the royal librarian, stood behind the dusty counter with a stern look. As Richard reached the front desk, the librarian gasped and ducked beneath the counter. Richard cleared his throat. "Umm…hello," he said. Suddenly, the woman reappeared, holding a small crossbow; her eyes narrowed in suspicion.

"Are you a Ruby guard or one of Quiller's henchmen?" she asked, the crossbow aimed directly at Richard.

"Easy, I was hoping this book could help me!" Richard said, his hands raised in a truce. "I'm no guard; just look at my cloak. I'm just looking to borrow this book." The librarian's name was Judy, her gaze unwavering; she lowered the crossbow but remained vigilant. "Okay, then. That will be one small ruby to borrow it for an octave."

Richard didn't know that Derek was Judy's former flame. Derek had visited the Royal Library numerous times to advance his studies of plants and gemotros for brewing. Back in the day, she and Derek would dine together and discuss books late into the night, often gossiping about his mentor Winston Fletcher, the realm's top brewmaster and scholar.

Richard, not having a ruby to offer, pondered for a moment. He then got an idea. He reached into his pocket, retrieving one of his crimson cigars. He placed it on the counter with a wry smile.

"How about a trade? This for the book?" he proposed.

The librarian eyed the crimson cigar, her scepticism momentarily lifting. After a moment's contemplation, she nodded. Realising now that Richard was a foreigner, she gladly handed him the book. She knew precisely what it contained; it was her way of helping the young bloke on his quest.

"You're going to need this, young man!" the librarian said as she recorded the book as *'on loan'*. She then placed the book on top of a folded blanket. "Reading by a campfire can be cold!"

"Thank you!" said Richard.

"One more thing, lad." Judy held out one of the library lanterns and handed it to him.

Richard left the library clutching the book, carrying an oil lantern for light and a heavy blanket for warmth. His steps were purposeful as he made his way back to camp within Crimson Forest.

At the camp, Richard saw Haley and Derek sleeping beside the warmth of the campfire. He sat down, then flipped through the pages of the old book, one by one. Richard then paused on the page that mentioned the secret passageway beneath the Ruby Palace and its dark history of the man who tunnelled it, Cranium.

Soon, Haley woke up. "What are you reading?" she asked.

"I'll tell you once Derek wakes up."

Not long after, Derek also woke up. Richard brought the group in close, clutching the old book. The anticipation in the air was thick as Richard started to explain his plan.

"Listen up, everyone," Richard began, his voice sharp. "We've got the key to the palace's secrets right here." He held up the ancient book, its frayed pages displaying maps of hidden passages and secret chambers.

"Our target is the royal food stores. It's time the Stephador Clan gave Ruby Town the food it deserves. We might need to borrow a few things from the palace." Turning to Derek, he asked, "Derek, can you brew something for our blades to make our cuts more effective?"

Derek, his mind already whirring with possibilities, replied, "Haley, let's gather Bloodcap Widows. We only need a couple for an ideal poison; they will need to be handled carefully."

Haley knew her mushrooms well, "Yes, I am not a dumb blonde, the widow maker is found under twisted tree roots; It's tricky, they've got a dark stem and gills. They take some finding. You know they were once used in an assassination attempt on Emperor Cranium himself."

"An assassination?" asked Richard.

Derek further added, "Yes, Cranium and the Emerald King met for lunch in Emedella to sign a non-aggression pact, a potential truce to border hostilities; however, Ruby Nation betrayed the deal, with the First Ruby War."

Haley then cut in and finished the story, "The Royal Ruby Guards had their blades dipped in toxin in case negotiations failed; however, King Jackale made all the Ruby guards hand in their blades at the fortress gates. The Emerald guards who handled the swords died, and Cranium later spun it as a failed assassination attempt on his life. I read too, Derek!" He was most impressed by Haley's knowledge. She then poked her tongue.

"Typical, and his son Maroon is no different, brew this poison!" Richard urged, "We need every advantage we can get!"

Derek quickly grabbed his portable cauldron from Haley's wagon and filled it with snow. Richard then turned to Haley. "Haley, I need you to go into town. Scout it out—make sure you note where the guards are lurking. We need to know their positions and strength."

Haley nodded. She had put on her cloak, which was also turned inside out to show as brown, as she headed towards the village.

A few hours passed...

Derek was hunched over the pot of bubbling brew atop the campfire, his brow furrowed in concentration. As Richard had ordered, a poison brewed from foraged mushrooms would be suitable to wipe down their swords—deadly edges that could help tip the scales in their favour. It would only take one cut to kill guards, and paralysis should set in within minutes, regardless of the size of the wound. It was a delicate process, and Derek was the expert in crafting such concoctions.

Derek looked up at Richard. His voice was urgent, "Richard, we're missing an ingredient. We need some Bandeira bush weeds or Emerald Pricks to finish the poison. Can you find some? I want this poison to be excruciating as well."

Richard nodded; both names referred to the same plant, and he set off. As he ventured through a maze of trees, his sharp eyes scoured every nook and cranny for any sign of the common Bandeira bush weeds amongst the snow. There, sprouting from a hollow log, was a cluster of plants that bore a striking resemblance to Derek's description. The plant looked green and healthy, with sharp, serrated leaves and tiny thorns.

He carefully plucked a handful of leaves.

It was at this moment that Richard made a strange discovery. As he removed the leaves from the Bandeira bush, a peculiar liquid started to ooze from the stem. It was a silvery, mercury-like substance, unlike anything he had ever seen. But, at the time, he didn't think much of it and kept gathering the leaves. He made his way back to Derek with the leaves in hand.

"Got them!"

As he neared the cauldron, his eyes locked onto Derek's eager gaze. With a confident flick, he tossed the leaves into the bubbling mixture. "Good on ya, Richard. I didn't reckon you'd find them so quickly. Usually, there aren't many in Crimson Forest," Derek replied.

But what happened next caught everyone off guard. The cauldron exploded and shot high into the air. The blast's force sent Derek and Richard reeling backwards, their ears ringing and their eyes wide with shock. The clearing was now a chaotic mess of broken glass, spilled ingredients, and a lingering, ominous fog. Haley had just returned from her scout mission. "Peroa! What happened?"

The aftermath left them in a state of stunned disbelief. Derek and Richard exchanged bewildered glances, searching for answers to the unexplained disaster. It was a chemical reaction Derek had never seen before. The cauldron was now on the ground, spilling an ominous blood-red puddle.

"Those weren't Bandeira bush weeds…"

Richard got up and brushed himself off. "Well… let's remake the poison!"

"Or we could give it a go? I reckon we've just found a new potion, maybe. We should at least see what it does," Derek pointed out.

"But what if it's dangerous? Or poisonous? This soup contains Bloodcap Widow and an unknown weed! I don't want to take that risk," Richard protested. "But it might not be," Derek said. Hesitantly, Richard retrieved a vial of the blood-red puddle and held it before his mouth.

"Are you sure about this?" Richard asked again, seeking reassurance. Derek nodded. Then a brave or incredibly stupid Richard took a sip. "It tastes a bit like… ruby wine?" Richard remarked.

"So, do you feel any different?" Derek asked.

"Not really." Suddenly, Richard disappeared into thin air, like a puff of smoke.

Derek looked around, confused. "Hey, where did you go?" he yelled, his gaze sweeping the campsite. Haley was also confused. Derek stood up, "Okay, very funny. Where are you hiding?" he called out, half-smiling. Richard tried to speak, but his words were muffled by the invisible barrier that cloaked him.

Derek's brow furrowed further as he kept searching. "Richard, this isn't the time for games," he said, his tone shifting between amusement and frustration.

After a few more seconds, Richard reappeared. The enchantment lifted, and he materialised once more amid the campsite. The air seemed to settle as the subtle distortion dissipated, leaving the clan members astonished.

"Richard, where were you?" Haley asked, her eyes wide with surprise. Derek, still processing what just happened, exclaimed, "Seriously? How did you…"

"I don't know," Richard replied, a sly grin now on his lips. "That potion sure is something special."

"Wait… so that potion just made you invisible?" Derek gasped.

"I think so!" Richard was convinced. Derek was amazed; they couldn't believe it.

"What was it like? What did you see?"

"Well, everything was weird… It was like my surroundings were all distorted. I tried to say something, but you two couldn't hear me."

"Fascinating," Derek remarked.

With a shared sense of awe and amusement at Richard's newfound brew, the Stephador Clan decided, as a joke, to playfully name the potion *'Richard's Wine'*.

The campfire slowly died as the sun was now high in the sky. The air was charged with anticipation as they prepared for the infiltration of the Ruby Palace. After nearly destroying his cauldron and himself, for that matter, Derek successfully concocted the poison for their blades. He also decided to brew one more, a little potion with what was left of his ingredients, a jar of Fazz Fire. Derek never shared this particular secret; however, it seemed to involve the crushing of some orange fungi and sulphur. He then handed around the group a bottle of poison to smother on their swords.

"We've got Richard's wine and some venom for our blades. The Ruby Palace won't know what hit it," was the final rallying cry from Richard.

At midday, the clan headed to the beach at Crimson Bay. Close to the fishing docks, they turned and approached the Ruby Palace walls, hoping no tower guards were watching the seaside. The plan was to use the wine once they were inside the palace. It would grant everyone temporary invisibility, allowing them to sneak around without being caught. Once they broke into the royal food store, they could take a heap of food for the starving folk.

"I have never heard of a back entrance to the Ruby Palace," Derek said, concerned. "I have," Richard said, glancing around cautiously. "I learnt about it this morning. There's a back entrance to the palace; follow me!"

Derek looked sceptical, "A secret entrance, are you sure about this?"

Richard nodded. They moved around the wall covering for about half a mile until they reached the spot marked on the map. Feeling along the back wall, Richard finally found a loose stone brick. Pushing it in, he heard a soft click, but nothing else happened.

"There must be a key, or mechanism, or secret lever, or something," Richard pondered.

"Maybe it can only be accessed from within," Haley suggested.

"No, it can be opened from here; I know it," Richard insisted. After some searching, Derek spotted a small flag from the Ruby Nation hidden in the grass.

"Look at this flag," Derek said. The flag depicted Emperor Cranium.

He lifted the flag; underneath it was a rusted crank handle covered in dirt. He turned it to the left. Suddenly, a deep rumbling echoed from behind them. The massive Ruby flag atop the palace started to move as if it were magically connected to the small flag in the grass. Before long, a stone door in the outer wall swung open, revealing the secret passageway.

"Woah, good job, Derek!" Richard exclaimed.

"Imagine the time it took to make that mechanism." Haley chuckled and said, "Paxta-Holla" as she lit the lantern with a fingertip.

Then they all stepped into the passageway. The narrow tunnel descended into the earth, much like a mine. The air was thick and stale, untouched by the outside world. The damp and cool walls bore the marks of labourious digging as if they held the secrets of a time long past. During the journey, Richard shared a ghost story in the dark about the passage and how it was built.

"Only a few know about this," Richard explained, ushering them along. "It leads straight to the dungeon. We'll be able to get in without being seen."

"Why does it lead to the dungeon?" Derek thought that wasn't a good place to start.

"Well, I've only just read about this secret passage this morning. The story is quite sad," Richard began. *'Many years ago, before Emperor Cranium was evil and took control of Ruby Nation, he was simply a peasant and a father. He was poor and stole food only to feed his family. One day, he was caught and confined to these dungeons' depths. In his cage, he resorted to desperate measures for freedom. With bare nails, he clawed at the earth tirelessly for many rotations, digging and tunnelling until he fashioned this passage, which we now walk through. Some say he went mad, while others believe that something triggered the darkness within him, and that's when the evil came to our realm. Folks say the god of death and war, Daradero, influenced him!'*

"That's not that sad," Haley scoffed. "Yeah, it is, think about it!" Richard snapped.

"Imagine clawing through the dirt and stone for rotations just to see your family again." Then they arrived. Emerging from the hidden passage, the group found themselves in the dungeon below the Ruby Palace. A rusty old cage sat atop an aged maintenance hole cover, hinting at its storied past. As they lifted the cover, the dimly lit dungeon unfolded before them.

They found themselves amidst a collection of old rusty cages and stone statues, each imprisoned and frozen. The dim candlelight cast eerie shadows, and the silence was profound as if the petrified figures held their collective breath. Large, thick dungeon candles could be seen, standing in pails lining a wall. One candle had now burnt down to a stump, creating a full pail of hot wax. It was well known that sometimes jailers would throw pails of hot wax over unfortunate souls.

"Woah...spooky." Haley gasped as she pointed to a statue of the well-known Realm Marshal Manor. He looked furious, but all Ruby folk knew him as a reasonable man, a voice of reason in the realm who stood for what is right.

"Indeed," Derek remarked.

One particular statue grabbed Richard's eye—a man with a blank expression and a hint of fear. Richard's fingers traced the man's stone-cold face through the bars of the cage. "This man, he's familiar to me."

Haley stared at the lifeless statue, her voice hushed. "He doesn't look very scared, considering he was about to be turned to stone." Derek, always the pragmatic one, examined the statue. "I think it's a bloke, maybe in his thirties or forties. He must have been a thief or miscreant."

Suddenly, Richard stepped in with an unsettling remark, "My father was no miscreant."

Everybody fell silent.

Richard was overwhelmed with a mix of emotions. "It's him, without a doubt." Derek looked at Richard, "But why is he here?"

With his gaze fixed on his father, Richard took a deep breath before recounting the tale. "My father and mother," he began, "had migrated to Ruby Nation many rots ago. My father was offered a job working for Emperor Maroon himself. I am unsure what he did exactly, but it was important."

Richard's voice trembled with both affection and sorrow, "A few octaves ago, he left for work and didn't return to our home in Banderian Village. Damian and I were so worried, and my mother… She believed he had abandoned us for palace maids." There was a deep ache in Richard's voice. His father's absence had influenced the chain of events, his mother's death during *The Night of the Long Spears*. He and Damian's whole perspective on his father's abandonment was wrong. Damian died thinking he had abandoned his family. Richard now faced the stone-hard truth in this forsaken dungeon.

"No, he didn't abandon us. It turns out he was just here, a statue in this rotten dungeon." He knew his father worked tirelessly every day, risking his life to ensure the family's well-being. He knew he loved his family deeply. Autumn Rallian was once again a hero in Richard's eyes.

Richard grabbed a crimson cigar from his top pocket and lit it with the Sapphire lighter, the ember casting a gentle, warm glow on his face before he took the first contemplative drag. A solitary tear then traced down his cheek, mingling with the flickering light from the dungeon candles.

"That's terrible!" Haley remarked.

Richard nodded, glancing at Derek, who was now thinking of his wife and children in Crimson Village. After taking a long drag, Richard seemed to have completely forgotten about what had just happened. He exhaled and, with a new seriousness, said, "Let's climb these stairs and finish this mission."

"Where do these stairs even lead to?" Derek asked.

Richard shrugged, "I guess we will have to find out; come on, let's go to the top." Just as Richard began ascending the narrow staircase, he stumbled, slipping on the very first step. He reached out to grab hold of something, but there was nothing, so he tumbled back down.

"Are you alright, Richard?" Haley extended her hand to help Richard to his feet.

"Ouch, I guess. Why did I slip?" Richard questioned, rubbing his head. Derek quickly investigated. "It appears to be candle wax on the steps; it hardened and made the stairs slippery."

"Who would do such a thing?" Richard groaned. He dusted himself off and cautiously continued. The stone walls were cold, and the dungeon smelled of dust mixed with an earthy, musty aroma that seemed to seep from everywhere. Thankfully, as they approached the top, the odour vanished and was replaced with the comforting fresh air.

At the top was a door, or what remained of one. Wooden debris lay scattered across the floor. Richard's fingertips brushed against the splintered doorframe as he entered the light. The words '... *goodbye to your mother*' were inscribed on a large wooden piece.

As the trio walked down a poorly lit dirt corridor, only a couple of lanterns and torches that lined the walls were alight. Ultimately, the corridor led them to what was a guardhouse for jailers. Blood-red light shone on the marble floor, a table, and the chairs. Pieces of mouldy cheese, soured crimson cider, and dirty plates were scattered over the table. Reatrit droppings were also evident, as the rodents had eaten food scraps. Blood was also visible on the table, and a sharpened set of shackles. "I don't like this place at all!" Haley gasped as she discarded her lantern.

"Shhh! We're in the jailor's guardhouse, and the palace halls are beyond that door. Keep your voice down! Now's a good time to take my wine," Richard whispered. Before they stepped through the door, Richard uncorked the potion, gas tingling at his nostrils. "Ready... one... two... three!" They all drank the potion at once.

As the potion took effect, the clan blended into the air around them, becoming invisible. They all stepped out into the open halls with a glance and a nod; they could see each other clearly as if they were in a new dimension.

"Let's go quickly," Haley whispered.

As they navigated the wide corridor, the trio moved with utmost caution. The red carpet beneath their feet muffled their footsteps, and the scent of the blood-red banners and wavire tapestries hanging from the arches lingered in the air. The palace was decked out to the nines with the Ruby Nation's flag, a constant reminder of the tyranny. The flag was familiar to all, as it was a centrepiece in every village.

The flag's primary colour was crimson, with a black shape in the centre depicting the silhouette of a fanged wavire, an uneasy reminder for the Stephador Clan. The wavire was the most well-known Ruby gemotro that struck fear into the nation, a useful symbol to show the emperor's power and rule. Perfect for the suppressive playbook if one wants to rule by fear.

Each step was a gamble. One sound could make the place echo like an ancient cathedral, and discovery could mean the whole mission went up in smoke.

Suddenly, Richard spotted two guards patrolling the dimly lit halls. The sound of their footsteps echoed loudly, ramping up the tension. Richard, leading the group, signalled for a pause. The clan could see and hear each other, but it was like they were in a shadowy realm where sight was obscured and noise seemed slowed. Their voices sounded as if they were underwater. Holding their breath, they waited for the guards to pass and then moved around the corner. But just as he thought he was safe, Richard turned the corner and abruptly found himself inches from a guard, standing tall.

He held his breath as the guard's nostrils flared and contracted, breathing like a snorting fernithor. The palace guard remained oblivious. Richard silently slipped past him.

"That was close," he whispered under his breath.

The clan kept going.

"Keep an eye out for anything that looks like food storage." Derek reminded.

Amidst the grandeur, Richard's curiosity was sparked by a door with the label *'Royal Ruby Museum'*. "Hey, let's look in there!" Richard suggested.

"I don't think the food storage is in there, Richard," Derek said. Richard couldn't resist the urge to investigate.

"Richard, we have to stay on track," Haley added.

Ignoring the warnings, Richard opened the door to the Royal Ruby Museum, revealing a grand room with paintings, golden statues, suits of gleaming armour, and ancient artifacts as centre pieces, all resting on pedestals inside glass casings.

"Woah…" Richard gasped, seeing the expanse of the museum stretching out before him.

Quietly closing the door, Derek also began touring the room, then he reminded them, "Come on, we don't have much time before this potion wears off."

The soft glow of sunlight bathed the room through red-stained glass windows, creating a gothic atmosphere. The first thing that caught his attention was two longswords resting on a pedestal within glass boxes. The inscription beneath the box read, 'The Blade of Wavires'. The second read 'The blade of Emperor Cranium, BlunderBee'.

"I have never heard of those weapons before," Richard remarked.

Adjacent to the first sword, a glass case was empty, its label reading 'Fossilised Sacro Selester Egg'. Another vacant pedestal bore the label 'Silver Apex'.

"Looks like a lot of these artifacts are missing for some reason," Richard observed, a confused expression on his face.

He continued his exploration, finding a glass case labelled 'Savata Feather' containing a long, pristine white feather. Paintings adorned the walls, depicting significant events in Ruby Nation's history – the coronation of Emperor Maroon, the turmoil of the First Ruby War, and countless other scenes that unfolded through the ages.

In a corner, they stumbled upon intricate tapestries woven with golden threads that told the story of ancient alliances and long-forgotten rivalries. A mysterious aura surrounded an empty pedestal labelled 'Alliance Contract', hinting at a relic of great significance that had vanished from the museum's collection.

Richard marvelled at the historical richness. The awe and reverence filled the air, and the artifacts whispered tales of triumphs and tragedies. Amidst the captivating lore, Richard's lost determination to find provisions for the village. His thoughts were momentarily overshadowed by curiosity. In the very centre of the museum stood a pedestal, larger and grander than the others. Engraved upon it were the words, *'Royal Ruby Crown, crafted for the cranium of Emperor Cranium'*.

Richard chuckled at the accidental pun on that label. This cabinet space was reserved for the crown; however, like many others, it was starkly empty, a void where the symbol of imperial power should have rested. Richard couldn't hide his disappointment.

"Well, this was a waste of time; why are there so many missing pieces? Did somebody steal them?"

Despite the awe-inspiring artifacts and their rich history, the absence of so many artifacts left a lingering sense of incompleteness.

Disappointed, Richard let himself out of the museum. "Finally," Haley uttered.

As they stepped back out into the grand palace corridor, a chill ran down Richard's spine. At some point, while exploring the museum, the invisibility potion lifted, and he turned to see a guard's eyes narrowing in suspicion. The invisible veil completely dissipated, and they were exposed. Panic seized the Stephador Clan, realising that their cover had been blown.

"Run!" Richard shouted, urgency in his voice. The trio sprinted through the palace, the grandeur of the halls now transformed into a maze. Guards' shouts echoed behind them, the clatter of an armoured pursuit growing louder.

"Halt!" ordered the royal guards. Derek glimpsed a door up ahead, signed *'Royal Food Stores'*. He expressed desperation, "We need to make it there, now!"

The guards were gaining ground. "Hurry!" Haley urged, clearly scared. With a final burst of energy, they reached the room and slammed the door shut, hastily barricading it with the provided drawbar. A drawbar was a defensive implement used to secure a castle door, handy for a room with valuable contents; it was fortunate for the Stephador Clan that these stores had such a locking mechanism.

Outside the room, the guards' shouts grew louder, and with each pound on the door, the situation intensified as they pondered how to get inside. "We can't stay here long," Richard panted, his mind racing. "We need to gather as much as possible and find another way out."

They found themselves in a colossal store filled with the bounty of the realm. Barrels of dried fruits, crates of bread, berries, racks of grombler meat, rare savanta meat, and an array of exotic fruits and vegetables adorned the room. The intoxicating aroma of abundance hung in the air, promising relief for the famine-stricken town.

"Haley," Richard ordered, "Help us gather as much as we can. We need to make this count."

Haley pulled out three big sacks from her shoulder bag. They filled them with the food treasures ahead, starting with rare Sapphire Blue cheese, the emperor's favourite. They rummaged through the many crates and barrels filled with tempting goods. The air was thick with the musty smell of aged grains and the earthy scent of root vegetables. As they hurriedly filled their sacks, the room echoed with the clink of metal ladles against wooden containers and the soft rustling of dried herbs.

"I'm stuffing a sack with ripe apples," Derek couldn't help but comment, "These are the juiciest I've ever seen!"

Haley reached for a wheel of cheese and added, "And the smell of this is amazing."

Richard, securing a bundle of herbs, couldn't suppress a grin. "The royal village will feast for days with beautifully roasted savanta meats." The clan's hands moved swiftly from one delicacy to the next. Barrels of lentils whispered promises of hearty soups while the sweet fragrance of honey drifted from a corner, tempting them to indulge. The colours of the fruits, bread, and cheeses created a rich and tasty scene before them.

Richard's eyes fell on a crate of fruits as they continued to fill their sacks. "Dried apricots and figs," he exclaimed. Amidst the bustling activity, the trio's laughter filled the air. The weight of all the visible spoils grew, and the storage room became a treasure trove of medieval flavours. Derek, catching sight of a crate of root vegetables, chuckled, "Turnips and carrots for everyone!"

Soon, the thumping grew fierce, and the guards tried to shoulder-charge the door to no avail.

Just as they were about to conclude their clandestine operation, Haley noticed a peculiar set of scrolls on a nearby table. "These seem important," she said, reaching out to grab them.

Curiosity sparked in Richard's eyes as she unravelled one of the scrolls. It had a sketch of a bowl filled with some rich stew. *'Royal Recipe: Secret Grombler noodles'*.

"It's a secret recipe; we have to take them!" Haley said, filled with enthusiasm. "No, I hate grombler. It's so chewy." Richard remarked.

"Look at this one!" Derek said, unravelling another scroll. This one had a sketch of a wooden stein with foam on the top, *'Royal Recipe: Sweet Crimson Cider'*. Just before the sacks became impossible to lift, they concluded the theft spree and turned to the following problem: a way out!

"Quick, we're running out of time!" Richard's eyes widened as the door hinges began to give in to the relentless guards.

In a quick, desperate move, Derek grabbed a jar from his pocket. "Everybody, come in close!" Derek shouted. As everyone huddled together, Derek threw the jar at his feet, calling, "Royal Ruby Library."

The jar shattered, releasing a burst of intense flames that consumed them. The clan was gone just as the door burst off its hinges, and guards entered the room. As if swallowed by a pillar of flames, Richard, Damian, and Haley vanished.

As the flames faded, the guards found a ransacked storage room. They then did what palace guards do best: they ate! The Ruby guards stuffed their faces. They devoured delicacies one after another, a far cry from the usual rations of ruby wine, porridge, and stale bread.

The clan materialised in the Royal Ruby Library, lugging three huge sacks of food. "Woah…" Derek remarked.

Gasping for breath, Richard and Haley exchanged wide-eyed glances. "Did we just teleport?" Richard asked. Still catching her breath, Derek explained, "Yep, it's lucky I brewed that small jar of Fazz Fire."

"Richard! You've returned!" the librarian exclaimed, her eyes wide with disbelief. Richard recognised her from this morning. "Yes, Judy," Derek said as he gave her a hug of more than just friendship. She now understood Richard was the leader of a clan. She grabbed a handbell from the counter and said, "Follow me!"

Judy led the clan back to the town square, ringing her bell and drawing a crowd all the while. People started to emerge and gather in the market square. A quiet excitement spread as they caught sight of the clan and the bounty they carried. It was as if the poor, starving folk could smell food.

Haley, reaching into the sacks, replied with a smile, "We've brought food. Enough to fill everyone's stomachs." With a heart of Peroa, she started to distribute the food.

"Don't forget to return that ancient book; secrets are priceless," Judy mumbled, mouthing down a royal cheese. "Now, would I forget you?" Derek added. Both Derek and Judy shared a strange connection, a pledge that would help record the moment of the Stephador Clan legend.

The news of the Stephador Clan spread like wildfire, and soon, the villagers, nearly all women and children, were queuing up to get something to eat. Yet no men were there, as it seems all had gone to join the Territorial Ruby Army Preparatory. Only a few old and frail men remained. Nonetheless, the air was filled with gratitude and relief, with words to the effect that Peroa herself had returned, clearly referring to Haley's beauty. "Peroa has returned," cried the children as they handed over the much-needed food.

Once they finished, Derek, his face beaming, patted Richard on the back. "You've become a hero, my mate, a King!" Richard, looking at the grateful faces around him, nodded. "This is for our village, for every person who has struggled. With Peroa's heart, we can weather any storm."

Richard's eyes shone with new hope as they neared the edge of the Crimson Forest. A sign hanging on a tree read:

WANTED
Richard Rallian - Leader of the Stephador Clan
Reward: 200 rubies

After noticing the sign, Derek chuckled, "Two hundred rubies isn't bad. I could turn myself in and get the reward for my wife and kids. Oh, dear, I mean daughter," he said, reflecting on the loss of his son. Richard lightened the situation, "Well, if they're offering that much, maybe we should all turn ourselves in." With a newfound hope, the clan vanished again into the forest, leaving the town's folk with full stomachs.

Chapter 6

Royal Treasury

Under the rustling canopy of Crimson Forest, the campfire flickered, its warm glow casting a soft light on the three gathered around it. The night air was filled with a tranquil hush, interrupted only by the occasional hoots from night-colaies. Haley and Richard were huddled under a blanket while Derek was reading the new crimson cider recipe, "Hmm, interesting." He began to read out loud.

How to brew Sweet Crimson Cider

Ingredients:

- 3 handfuls of fresh crimson berries
- 4 tufts of Bandeira Bush weeds
- 1 cup of sugar
- 1 cup of ruby wine
- 6 cups of water
- 1 steel pot
- mortar and pestle
- 1 leaf of aztel fern

Method:

1. Place the crimson berries, sugar, and aztel leaf in a mortar and pestle. Pound into a paste.

2. Boil the ruby wine and Bandeira bush weeds in the pot for 1 hour.

3. After simmering for 20 minutes more, transfer the crimson berry paste into the pot with the boiled wine.

4. Stir thoroughly, then put out the flame and let it simmer on coals for 8 hours.

5. Dilute with 6 cups of water.

6. Mix thoroughly again, then strain the broth into a bottle. Discard the remaining sludge. Let the brew rest for an octave before opening.

7. Serve and enjoy.

"That sounds like a very complex recipe," Haley remarked. Then Richard stood and started barking orders.

"Okay, everybody, we must create a few crimson-oil cocktails tonight."

"What for?" Haley asked. Richard then met her gaze. "Food just isn't enough for them. Folks need more. We must infiltrate a place even more protected and fortified than the palace, the Royal Treasury. Once we are in, we can give away the emperor's wealth, every last ruby."

"Okay, is there anything I can do?" Derek was eager to help. Richard paused for a moment.

"There is one thing."

Later, in the middle of the night…

In the heart of the royal town's square stood the grand statue of Maroon in heroic pose, holding BlunderBee, the longsword—a blade forged long ago by the blacksmiths of Gorlith. The sword was welded by his father, Cranium, during the first Ruby War. The statue towered as a symbol of the emperor's unwavering rule, a reminder to all of the realm's oppression. However, there was a flaw with it; the emperor's imperfections were sculpted right down to his rather skinny and unsteady legs.

The Stephador Clan encircled the sculpture, their silhouettes flickering in the moonlight. "Ready?" Richard called out, "Now!"

With skill, they tossed ropes at the statue, lassoing it around its neck.

"NOW PULL!" Their ropes were taut, and their muscles strained. The imposing monument slowly began to shift. It groaned and creaked as if the stone itself was protesting the erosion of its tyrannical might. It hadn't left its pedestal for over a decade, but now was its time; now was its end.

A small crowd holding lanterns gathered to watch in awe and

anticipation. Every eye was locked on the figure of Maroon, teetering precariously on its stone base. The folk in the square held their collective breath, awaiting the inevitable.

And then, it happened—the statue shifted, and the right leg snapped at the knee. With a resounding crash, the statue tumbled to the ground, shattering into a cloud of chalky pieces. The oppressive symbol crumbled easily; it wasn't made of solid stone but was sculpted from cheap materials. The square echoed with the rebels' triumphant roars and the people's cheers. "I love it when a plan comes together!" Richard proudly grinned.

As the crowd cheered, the smell of a fresh cigar drifted from his top pocket. Derek, covered in chalky dust, patted Richard on the back. "You did it, Richard! We've shown them that tyranny won't stand!" Amidst the dust and the victorious cheers, Richard, the embodiment of unwavering defiance, retrieved another cigar from his pocket. Richard was now full of adrenaline. He proclaimed, "We've only just begun. This is a message to oppressors everywhere. Change is coming." With his defiant act complete, Richard took a solitary step away from the crumbled sculpture. He rolled the Sapphire lighter with his thumb and lit up his sixth crimson cigar, a growing habit over the past days, and took a long, well-deserved drag. The bittersweet taste of smoke filled his mouth and drifted out through his nostrils.

"That's the good stuff," Richard said as he blew smoke into the air. He then turned his eyes towards the fortified Royal Treasury building nestled beside the market square. The air was thick with anticipation as the clan stared at their next target. Guards started to pour out of the building, over a dozen royal guards.

Richard, his eyes shining with resolve, produced the prepared crimson-oil cocktails. "Ready yourselves, light 'em up," he ordered. "This is our moment."

Derek placed the few bottles on the ground. Haley held out her hand at the oil-soaked wicks.

"Paxta-Holla!" The cocktails were ready.

With calculated precision, the flaming cocktails soared through the night sky, smashing into the unsuspecting guards. A sudden burst of flames erupted, followed by explosions. Two disoriented guards scrambled amid the chaos, trying to extinguish the fire that engulfed their comrades. Seizing the moment, the Stephador Clan charged at the building, swords drawn. Only one tall guard stood posed at the treasury entrance. Then swords clashed, and the night echoed with the sound of metal against metal.

"Keep him busy!" Richard yelled, his sword slashing through the air. Caught in a defensive struggle, the remaining guard dropped his weapon.

With a cigar in his mouth, Richard then approached the imposing vault doors. He conjured his spell with a flourish, his hands raised and moving in the practised dance. "Hella-scaren-peta-shingo," he intoned, casting a spell that resonated fire with wind.

The massive doors, adorned with intricate engravings, groaned and shuddered as a fierce tornado of flames forced them wide open with a resounding boom. The economic heart of the Ruby Nation was laid bare, with piles of rubies shimmering like molten embers in the vault's light. Flames licked the stone walls, engulfing anything that could burn. Wooden chests, furniture, and tapestries all caught alight. However, with no way to escape, the tornado quickly died down, flinging its final flames back onto the massive treasury doors, which were now also aflame.

"Look at this," Derek exclaimed, his eyes widening. "We've hit the motherlode!"

Haley smirked. "It's time to redistribute this wealth."

Richard raised his hand as the clan marvelled at the vast riches. "Let's not forget why we're doing this. It's for them," he nodded towards the market square. "Let's give them a taste of what the emperor has hoarded."

Together, they worked quickly, sacking and then distributing the wealth to any eager hands that night who had gathered in the square. Floods of village women and children started to help themselves to the treasury hoardings. Rubies cascaded like a torrent among the crowd, and the once-starving inhabitants revelled in the newfound prosperity. Laughter and cheers echoed through the night as the Stephador Clan, a band of outlaws, stood alongside the women and children, sharing in the triumph over oppression.

"We did it!" Derek cheered.

Celebrations in the village square carried on, while those in the palace prepared for a reprisal. Soon, the cheerful mood was suddenly broken as a distinct marching sound reached their ears. A cold realisation dawned on the Stephador Clan as the elite Corporal of the Palace Guard, along with his heavily armed men, wielding long, sharp spears and pavises, emerged from the palace doors.

Haley's eyes narrowed, and she shot a worried glance at Derek. "We've got company, and they don't look friendly."

Sensing the sudden shift in the air, the villagers fled with their newfound wealth. The revelry ceased, replaced by a palpable tension as the reinforcements advanced in a coordinated battle line. Richard, caught off guard, felt a surge of panic. The sight of the long spears and pavises sent shivers down his spine, triggering haunting flashbacks from *The Night of the Long Spears*. The spectre of those traumatic memories still loomed large, and he could feel the weight of dread settling over him.

Without saying a word, Richard signalled the clan to retreat.

He was suddenly overwhelmed by anxiety and needed to leave, distance himself, gather his thoughts, and quell the rising tide of emotions threatening to engulf him. Haley realised his distress and called after him, "Richard, where are you going? We need to face them together!" But Richard, lost in the echoes of the past, couldn't bring himself to respond. He ran! Soon, Haley and Derek both realised it was foolhardy to stay and fight; the enemy was far too strong. They slipped amongst the villagers to make their escape, still with a sack of loot.

Back at the camp, Richard huddled under his blanket; he was having an emotional breakdown. It wasn't until Haley found him that he sat back up. Understanding that he needed time, Haley decided to rekindle the fire, hoping the new warmth would help calm Richard down. The night air was cool, and a gentle breeze whispered through the crimson trees as Haley sat by Richard. She was as calm as Peroa herself, comforting him as they watched the fire dance.

"Whatever is bothering you, Richard, just know we are here for you." Suddenly, Richard's expression changed. He cleared his throat, catching Haley and Derek's attention.

"Guys, I think this is the end," Richard said, rising from a hypnotic trance caused by watching the dancing flames. "The Stephador Clan has peaked. We have pillaged the Ruby Treasury, upturned an armoured caravan, raided the royal food stores, and crumbled the emperor's statue. We have achieved our goals."

Haley and Derek exchanged glances, their expressions a mix of surprise and concern. The fire crackled, its warmth mingling with the cool forest breeze.

"What are you trying to say, Richard?" asked Haley, her voice tinged with uncertainty.

"Well, I'm on my last crimson cigar," Richard admitted, his gaze fixed on the fire.

Haley stepped in, her concern evident. "But we can't stop now. I still have so much to do! I am so full of ambition; I want Maroon to feel the wraith of HAVOC… Richard. I can't just leave the clan."

"You can never leave the clan, you will always be part of the clan, you too, Derek," reassured Richard. "Ok… guys, I have one final plan. It'll be a finale to be remembered throughout Gemotroplis."

"How?" Derek asked.

"We will need a lot more crimson oil…gallons," replied Richard.

Understanding Richard's proposition, Derek nodded and said, "I am onto it". Visions of his lost son filled him with vengeance.

The next morning, as the first light of dawn painted the Crimson Forest in hues of red, Richard, anxious, decided to take a solitary walk. The campfire was now just smouldering embers. As he wandered deeper into the forest, he came across a clearing bathed in dappled sunlight. In the centre stood an enigmatic statue of a boy, untouched by time. The boy's expression held a sense of innocence with a warm smile. The boy stood beside an old water well, the stones weathered by many rots gone by.

Richard couldn't help but wonder how such a statue found its place in this secluded part of the forest. What stories did it hold? What memories were etched into its stony features? Driven by curiosity, Richard approached the well. He took a ruby from his pocket, a small piece of the stolen treasury, and tossed it into the depths. The echoing clink against the stone walls marked its fall.

"What did you wish for?" Haley's voice interrupted the serene atmosphere as she appeared beside him.

"Can't tell you, it would ruin it," Richard chuckled, a sombre look in his eyes. Haley raised an eyebrow, a playful smirk forming on her lips. "A secret wish, huh? Well, I hope it brings you everything you desire."

"Me too, but I don't believe in wishing wells. It's all a lot of nonsense, but it's a nice idea." Haley then moved closer, wrapping her arms around Richard from behind; her beautiful presence and the gentle touch of her bosom calmed him.

"I wonder what's down there?" Richard remarked, gazing into the well.

"Maybe there's a monster, something that steals all the rubies that are thrown in," whispered Haley, as she deliberately blew on the back of his neck.

Then their eyes met, and they shared a kiss; the two discovered love with Haley leading the way! They rolled around among the grass and leaves.

An hour passed…

Richard, now much calmer, extended his hand and helped Haley to her feet. "All right, we'd better get back to Derek. We need to start work on my new plan."

"Okay, so what do we need to do?" Haley asked.

"Well, I need to grab a few things from the sea market down by the docks, and in the meantime, we need to gather as much crimson oil as we can."

Later that morning, the sun hung low over the horizon, casting a warm glow on the beach sands as Richard headed towards the dock. The rhythmic lapping of waves from Crimson Bay played against a small fishing boat tied to the pier. As he got closer, the smell of fish and brine filled the air. He entered the only seaside hut, where a frail fisherman lived and sold and pickled his catch. Inside, he saw many small barrels of sardines, their scales shining in the light, with a couple of larger barrels holding his nets behind him.

Richard sauntered up to the fisherman, who was sitting practising knots with a piece of rope and a float. "Can I buy a large barrel?" he inquired, pointing at the barrels behind the man. The fisherman, taken aback, blinked in surprise. "A barrel?" His weathered face reflected his confusion.

Richard nodded confidently. "Yes, a barrel!"

"Alright then. That'll be 30 small rubies," he said, considering the unusual request.

"No, no, no… I want a large barrel, not the fish," Richard clarified. The fisherman scratched his head, puzzled by how strange the situation was. Sensing he needed to persuade the fisherman, Richard reached into his pocket and pulled out his WANTED poster. He unrolled it on the table as if it were a prized piece of art.

"So, if I turn you in to the emperor… he will give me 200 fat rubies?" the fisherman asked, squinting at the poster as if trying to figure out what Richard was telling him.

"That's right," Richard said confidently, "Are you with me or are you not?"

The tired old fisherman had no time for enemies or friends; he simply sought peace. He was the one feeding the village for years with his sardines; he smelled the flames and heard the spectacle from the village last night.

"Son, I don't care for rubies; I seek peace and quiet for my beloved town. Please just take my barrels," replied the fisherman.

After a quick chat, Richard left the market with the big barrel on his back and some smaller ones stacked within. That was just the first step. Still, there were many tasks to complete before his plan could be put into motion.

Derek and Haley had been working tirelessly together, gathering ingredients from the forest, such as crimson berries and tapping sap from crimson trees. They shared their secrets, potion recipes, and inventions. Derek even showed Haley that crimson oil could be more easily extracted from large, crystallised chunks, which could be simply crushed to release the oil reserves inside. They easily filled the wagon with such large sap crystals, with one especially massive crystal holding nearly a pint of oil. Derek's idea had significantly reduced their workload.

That night around the campfire, while Richard and Haley slept, Derek was so dedicated; he journaled the story of the Stephador Clan in full, using the back pages of the ancient book 'The Ruby Palace'. He scribed the clan's mantra, the discovery of Richard's Wine, and added the scrolls of Haley, the blueprints of a better world, knowing only too well the purpose of the clan's finale. With the final stroke of his quill, he titled his leader King Richard. "Yes, he is a Topaz King," thought Derek, a true leader of the Topaz people and this clan.

Emperor Maroon would soon find out about the clan's success at breakfast.

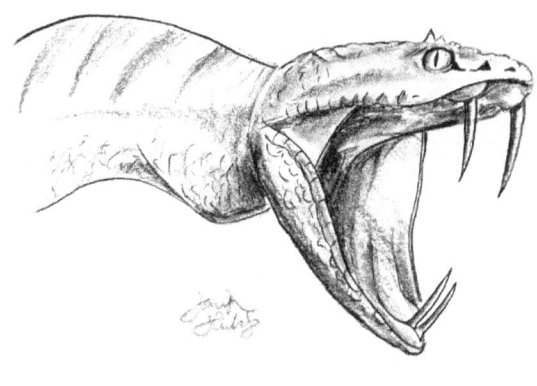

Chapter 7

Ruined Breakfast

Emperor Maroon awoke at dawn, yawning and rubbing his eyes in bed. He was lying on a grand carved wooden bed with matching nightstands. His bedroom was a large chamber at the top of the highest tower in the Ruby Palace. His servants had embroidered his name onto the bedsheets, pillows, and covers as constant reminders of his importance. This was necessary because Maroon appreciated these simple gestures, valuing that others took the trouble to label his belongings. Without them, he found it hard to sleep well, which could harm the realm. Servants even went so far as to sew his name onto his underwear and socks, which he kept in the top drawer of his nightstand alongside other treasured items.

He chose his pentagonal bedchamber, which had windows on each wall, allowing him to survey the horizon in all directions. He enjoyed gazing out of these windows, hand on chin with a blank, expressionless face. He often looked at the border mountains over Crimson Forest or out to Crimson Bay, depending on what was bothering him. During these moments of contemplation, he cleared his mind, which helped him plan his next moves. However, this morning was a little different. As he walked towards the most southern-facing window, he could hear the regular chirping of colaies, mixed with the lively singing of children from the town square below. He wasn't used to hearing happy sounds, and it unsettled him, as his approach was to rule through fear.

"What on Gemotroplis is going on? This does not seem right! I'll ask Quiller over breakfast." With that, he shut the window tight, drowning out the bloody racket, and headed down the spiral staircase in his crimson silk pyjamas. With each step, his stomach was growling, a noise magnified by the echo of the tight and steep stone steps.

"I need a good breakfast!" Maroon whispered to himself, knowing that his temper could sometimes get the best of him, especially if he weren't well-fed.

"The kitchen servants and Quiller had better be on the ball this morning."

The breakfast chamber was also a grand space, featuring a long, intricately carved dining table surrounded by many luxurious red chairs. Maroon preferred solitude and enjoyed the quiet; as a result, the room or palace rarely saw much activity. At the far end was the emperor's chair, positioned in front of a stained glass window that showed a knight bearing the Ruby Nation emblem on his red shield, the wavire.

Emperor Maroon pulled back the chair and sat down. "Quiller! Why isn't my breakfast ready?" Quiller, his top servant, was in charge of having his breakfast prepared, placed, and ready, along with the royal newspaper, for the morning routine. Maroon hated breaking routine nearly as much as he hated all foreigners.

"Quiller, I am so hungry, I could eat a savanta."

Breaky usually consisted of his favourite Sapphire Blue, the exotic imported cheese, lovely fruit, and a golden goblet of crimson cider.

"Heil, Emperor Maroon, and a good morning. Breakfast is served," proclaimed Quiller with his head down as he rushed in carrying the silver breakfast tray. It took more than a moment of awkwardness for Quiller to traverse the length of the long table. Quiller finally placed the silver tray in front of Maroon, which held a goblet of ruby wine, a bowl of sloppy hot porridge, and stale bread.

"What is this slop, Quiller? Where is my crimson cider and cheese – Sapphire Blue!" Maroon slammed his fist onto the table.

"The crimson cider recipe has been stolen, sire!"

"What! You knuckleheads did not make a spare copy?" Maroon said, having to raise his voice. The village children's joyous singing outside the breakfast chamber window grew louder, making Maroon uneasy.

"No, sire."

Realising he needed to justify his actions quickly, Quiller grew nervous.

"It's standard rations for the Ruby Army: ruby wine, hot porridge, and bread. It's all that's available this morning…sire."

"What, not even some crimson berries for this porridge puke!"

"No, sire."

Maroon was disgusted but hungry, so he begrudgingly started eating it, spoonful by spoonful. Slowly and painfully, like it was a bowl of hot steaming vomit, screwing up his face and having to blow each spoonful.

SLURP

As Maroon struggled with the porridge, trying to mouth down the slop, Quiller took the opportunity to explain.

"Sire, the palace stores were raided by a renegade clan, and your precious cheese stocks are all gone, and as mentioned, the cider recipe was stolen. I only received our royal guard's notification this morning. Sire, I only first became aware of this when I picked up your breakfast tray."

Maroon was beginning to lose it…

"Why wasn't I briefed on this, Quiller? We had barrels of cider!" Maroon was clearly concerned about his cheese and the lack of cider.

"Sire, you have been in bed for three days, recovering from your birthday bash. You and the royal guards drank the last of our cider right in this very chamber," Quiller reminded Maroon.

"Yes, Quiller, now that was a party!" Maroon raised his goblet of ruby wine as if his mood instantly switched to a more joyous one.

"At least I will be eating breakfast like a true emperor, better than those noisy villager children outside that window," he scoffed with a laugh.

"Bring me the Royal Newspaper…"

Maroon, every octave, received a *State of the Nation* report at breakfast, which he called his newspaper. Quiller clapped his hands and motioned to a servant standing outside the doors. The royal servant, carrying a red cushion on top of a bent hand above his head, rushed in, stopping right in front of Quiller. The *Royal Newspaper* was an official scroll written on parchment, which was used to preserve the realm's news and record the fines and taxes imposed by other nations. It was an official document in which the emperor's actions were justified—a final journal, like heavily redacted meeting minutes. The scroll's final destination was delivery to the royal librarian for the archives. This was the way the palace recorded all the reparations enforced by other nations after the First Ruby War.

Quiller nervously lifted the scroll from the red cushion. Taking a few steady steps back, he unrolled the newspaper and began reading it in his best newsreader voice, trying to keep the message upbeat.

"Hurry up, Quiller, or the dungeon's waiting for you. Shall I remind you this breakfast slop sucks?" mouthed Maroon, half choking on a spoonful.

"The People's Opinion, sire."

Quiller explained that all recruitment flyers had been distributed by airdrop using the Royal Sacro Selester. All males had been ordered to join the Territorial Ruby Army Preparatory for enlistment and training.

"Nationwide compliance is acceptable, sire. Colonel Manor has reported that hundreds of men are entering the army camps in Bandeira."

"What about the foreign folk?"

"All have been dealt with through either internment or other means, as requested. Sire, Henry IronShard, the master blacksmith, has recently been coerced into only forging weapons for the Ruby Army."

"Excellent, Quiller!"

"Sire, regarding that recent uprising in Banderian Village…." Quiller introduced.

"Yes, I remember that old news, Quiller. I hear that my favourite statue's wife started it." Maroon was referring to the statue of a Topaz employee now in his dungeon. "What's her name? Wait! There's no need to respond, Quiller. Her name does not matter anymore. Was she dealt with?"

"Yes, sire."

"Sire, regarding the recent uprising in Crimson Village…" Quiller repeated.

"Crimson Village… That one is new!" Maroon raised an eyebrow.

"Sire, the uprising in Crimson was due to starving villages and the recent markets being destroyed by a firestorm. We suspect Topaz terrorists were responsible."

Maroon said firmly, "Did my guards deal with them?"

"Yes, sire. All Topaz foreign men and boys."

"Excellent work, good job, Quiller." Maroon then chugged back some ruby wine.

My realm, Quiller, is running perfectly, apart from those blasted kids singing outside that window," Maroon cheekily bragged.

"Now, move on to finances for the Ruby Army Preparatory," said Maroon, glaring deep into Quiller's eyes.

Quiller was now clearly shaken, realising that the rest of the royal news was not as pleasant. He took a few more steps back, his hands trembling over the scroll. The terrible news was still to come. Maroon could sense it, like a wavire on the hunt for prey. He felt the air shifting. Quiller knew the emperor loved to shoot the messenger.

"Hurry, Quiller, my dungeon needs filling."

"The emperor of Topaz Nation has not taken lightly your refusal to pay his ten thousand large rubies tax, restitution from the First Ruby War."

"So what? It is part of my grand plan, Quiller. We are going to need every last ruby to pay the Ruby Army. I am not paying that knucklehead."

"Our scouts inform us he is readying for war; one thousand ferinthor cavalry have been sighted in Areden, that's just a stone's throw from Ravena, sire."

"So, he's gearing up for a fight! Anyway, how's the ruby production going?"

"Ruby production in the mines is down, sire. Our young lads are struggling. The mine's locomotive has broken down, and all stone and rock must traverse the great stairs on their backs."

"Increase production, make them work nights. Use foreigners as miners if you need to!"

"Yes, sire." Quiller was now uncontrollably shaking. "One more matter, the last ruby caravan to the Royal Treasury was lost…"

"How do you lose a caravan? Those pelatas are massive beasts," yelled Maroon as if Quiller were personally responsible. With that, Maroon slammed his goblet of ruby wine, spilling the bowl of hot porridge down his royal crimson pyjamas. Maroon jumped out of his chair, slightly burned. Quiller thought that the emperor was going to throttle him. Quiller was about to run, but Maroon only reached for a napkin and started to wipe the porridge off his pyjamas.

"Two young Topaz boys hijacked the caravan, sire."

"I thought you said all Topaz boys were liquidated. I hate those Topaz reatrits!" Maroon was still wiping himself with the napkin.

"No, sire. I said dealt with. Good news, in any case, we know the culprit, one Richard Rallian. I have wanted posters now all over Ruby Nation looking for him." Quiller tried to calm the emperor by showing that a solution was already in place.

Maroon then looked at Quiller and said, "Rallian, Rallian, why is that name familiar?"

"It's the name of Autumn Rallian, your past Topaz employee," Quiller explained.

"Who?"

"Your favourite statue in the dungeon." Quiller provided the clarity.

"Oh yes!" Maroon laughed, then laughed again, and again, growing louder, until instant rage took hold. Maroon lost control and began thrashing his breakfast tray. The remaining porridge and ruby wine flew in all directions.

"What the hell!" Maroon was ready this time to cast Quiller straight into the dungeon. Just before Emperor Maroon was about to bark the order, the Corporal of the Palace Guard interjected into the breakfast chamber.

"What's this disruption?" Maroon yelled, turning his pointed finger away from Quiller, now clearly accusing the corporal. He hated being interrupted during his morning newspaper, especially when he was having breakfast and particularly at this embarrassing moment, in porridge-soaked pyjamas.

Off the big tabletop, more plops of porridge and a flow of ruby wine hit the floor. Maroon then slipped and fell on his backside. Those unlucky souls in the room could see the anger in his eyes. Quiller was careful not to laugh and was grateful for the corporal's interruption.

This particular corporal had only just gained some favour with Maroon and was promoted to Corporal of the Palace Guard. Last octave, he reported events from the border wall in Bandeira. Maroon considered him a potential replacement for Quiller, as he appreciated his prudent honesty and down-to-earth approach.

"Sire, your royal monument in the town's square has been toppled, and the Royal Treasury has been raided. All your rubies are now lost!" reported the corporal.

Maroon ran his wine-soaked, porridge-ridden hands through his dark hair. This was the one time he was lost for words. The corporal further elaborated. "Children are also having a lavish breakfast and singing songs in the royal town square, sire. Praising a young man named Richard Rallian, and that Peroa has returned. Just ask this boy!" The corporal then dragged a boy by the collar as evidence. The corporal shoved the young boy and his crimson berry-stained shirt into the room. He was still eating his breakfast, munching on some Sapphire Blue cheese in one hand and the most beautiful red apple in the other. The red apple was to die for!

Maroon stood carefully, trying to gather some dignity, wiping away rare tears with his porridge-soaked hands. He stood and began walking up to the boy, attempting to show authority. Maroon then grabbed the cheese out of the boy's hand.

"What's your name, son?" asked Maroon.

"Nathan," replied the young lad of only thirteen rots.

"Now tell me about this Richard Rallian," Emperor Maroon asked in a pleasant voice. Maroon was only now settling down, as he finally had some precious Sapphire Blue cheese.

"Oh, Richard Rallian and his clan are heroes fighting for our freedom. Richard Rallian will return as a stephador. He is the creation of Peroa!" the boy responded in song. Then the boy took a big bite of his apple and continued to munch away, finally adding, "Oh Peroa, yes, she is as beautiful as is her heart."

Maroon knew the stephador was Topaz Nation's emblem, symbolising a foreign power uprising within his own Ruby Nation. This situation was tough to swallow, like the dammed porridge, with all this now happening in the heart of Royal Ruby Town.

"Take that boy out of my sight, his joyous nature makes me sick!" ordered Maroon. With that, the corporal saluted and left, escorting the young lad back down the long corridor, ready to chuck him down the palace stairs and into the town's square.

Maroon turned to face Quiller, "I am going to change my clothes, bathe, and then we can resume the royal news with some dignity upon my return." Maroon began to climb the stairs to freshen up, and servants started a flurry to organise warm water for his tub, which was high up in the bedroom chamber. Quiller and other servants took the time to tidy up the disastrous breakfast mess.

After a short while, a clean, calm, well-dressed emperor in full robes of authority re-entered the breakfast chamber. "Begin, Quiller!" he ordered.

Knowing it was time to turn to some real good news and repair the morning's debacle, Quiller started. "Royal Army numbers are up, sire…"

"Yes, Quiller, we have covered that!" spinning around to face him. Quiller again kept a healthy distance.

"Hundreds of men have signed up for Ruby Army Preparatory duty. Food and weapon stores are looking good, but the army will need long-term payment and feeding. Only three quintets of food stores are estimated to remain, and no trade is occurring, so taxes are down. All able-bodied men have joined the army, and our markets and farm production have come to a standstill. The roads are empty of traders. Topaz, Emerald, and Sapphire foreigners are all fleeing due to our recent crackdowns. Those caught are branded with a hot iron and then placed in camps for training or to help work the farms and mines."

Quiller was trying to put a positive spin on the situation and plant some solutions in Maroon's mind to ease any further mood swings that might result in his imprisonment. Maroon, clearly more settled after his royal bubble bath, was still troubled by the singing of villagers from the town square. He walked to a large arched stained-glass window and saw the joyful crowd picnicking on his toppled statue. The emperor stood there, contemplating, his arms crossed for a minute, with his back turned.

"While having a bath, I have had time to think, Quiller. Yes, you will run the farms like the mines. Furthermore, use those internment camps for weapon production. We will need a workforce," Maroon said, now owning Quiller's proposal.

Not known to Maroon, Quiller had already put such production measures in place.

"We need total commitment from our Ruby Nation. Every man, woman, and child must commit to this war effort, Quiller!"

"Yes, sire."

"Put that Ruby Town ramble down there, those outside this window to work. The fate of this nation is in the hands of its people." Maroon then turned to face Quiller.

"Also, conscript that young Nathan, he cannot be gloating at me, his singing is driving me crazy."

"Yes, sire."

Maroon loved to evade responsibility or shift blame to others if the outcome was in doubt or something annoyed him. He then waved to another servant, "Keep those bloody doors open. I need fresh air. This room smells of porridge!"

Quiller motioned to the servant, who then secured the doors wide open.

With the large chamber doors now fully open, the emperor glimpsed the corporal returning from the town square. The sight jogged Maroon's vengeful memory. "And for those guards that have let down team Maroon, particularly those running that treasury caravan. Send them to the front, straight into battle as fodder, Quiller!" ordered Maroon.

"Ok, the guards have been found. They were drunk at Tether's Tavern. Still, they're just old blokes nearing retirement, and the war hasn't even kicked off yet," Quiller added.

"Are you questioning me, Quiller? What do you expect of me, Quiller? Should I promote them for their duty well served? Seriously, Quiller," Maroon started to rant, but in a calm, emotionless voice.

"Quiller... yes, let's reward all the incompetent fools in the realm and let them lead our ranks into battle. Okay, great idea, Quiller!" Maroon then added, "I understand we are down a captain or two. Promote those old carriage guards as you have suggested and put them on the border wall; those sacro slithers still need taming."

Maroon has just recalled the briefing of a recent battle, a newspaper report the corporal gave last octave. It was a memorable morning, a breakfast of Sapphire Blue cheese and crimson cider, a morning when the 'Royal Newspaper' was acceptable. The news that day was just some minor destruction of towers, some guard deaths, and the loss of the Captain of the Guard due to the flying sacro slithers in Bandeira. A pleasant briefing when all was in control. That's why he respected or at least listened to the corporal; he was a structured, disciplined military man, a man of no political spin, who was explaining his encounters with a young boy called Lustre. No porridge was spilled that morning.

"Now, where were we with my newspaper? Get to the point," ordered Maroon.

"The matter of Richard Rallian and the Stephador Clan sire."

Maroon glared with an apparent madness in his eyes, a crazy stare. Quiller broke the awkward silence with this clarification. "Sire, all this mayhem is because of Richard Rallian…"

"Yes indeed, it is Quiller, that Topaz scum! Quiller, get me my father's sword, BlunderBee, and my new battle dress with Irisavire; I will deal with this Richard Rallian personally." Maroon showed a clenched fist.

"And the jewel, sire!"

Maroon then said quietly, lowering his voice so no servants could hear. "Of course, you fool, the Heart of Gemotronia shall never leave my side. Where is it anyway? I will need it to deal with this Richard and this so-called goddess Peroa."

"I assume it's in your nightstand's underwear and socks drawer, sire."

"Thanks, Quiller. Get me my father's blade, it will again taste Topaz blood." Maroon then resolutely left the room and ascended the stairs towards his bed chamber to gather the Heart of Gemotronia.

Quiller's royal duty now was to promptly record the chaotic morning's events, redact any sensitive or embarrassing details, and give the officially signed journal to the Royal Librarian, Judy, as a record of the official briefing.

Quiller took a deep breath; he knew that he had barely escaped the dungeon and that he was still not out of the woods with the yet-to-be-drafted journal. This newspaper journal was going to take some crafting, he thought. Quiller's job was filled with risks that could lead to his imprisonment. He left the room, entering the Royal Ruby Museum to gather Cranium's sword, BlunderBee.

Chapter 8

The Finale

It was mid-morning. Haley and Derek were checking the wagon and running through the plan when Richard approached.

"Ok, let's do this!" he said, raising his fist in the air.

Haley had left the bag with her blueprints beside the campfire. Derek, noticing this, picked up the bag and put it into the wagon. Then the men began to haul the wagon towards Royal Ruby Town.

The trio gathered on the outskirts of town. It was midday, and the air was thick with anticipation as they huddled together to discuss the plan one last time. Haley, her eyes focused and resolute, took a deep breath and said, "Alright, here's the plan. I'll gather a crowd and lead them to the palace doors—the main entrance with the two black statues. We, the village folk, will then request a meeting with the emperor. I can charm the pants off any guards with my smile and convince the emperor to come outside to negotiate. Let's use our hoardings from his Royal Treasury as bait."

Richard nodded, "There's nothing like reclaiming his lost wealth to entice. I'll keep watch from a distance. If anything goes wrong, I'll intervene. Just stay alert, Haley. If possible, I need to meet the emperor alone without crowds." Richard then kissed Haley on the forehead.

Derek, gripping the wagon harness, looked at them both. "And I'll be pulling the precious cargo, right?" He understood Richard's true intentions. Richard then patted the large barrel on the wagon.

"Yes, it's our final act, and we must execute this perfectly."

Haley glanced at the wagon and then back at Richard. She closed with, "Remember, we're doing this for the people of the Royal Ruby Town who suffer under Maroon's rule. This is our chance to make a real difference." She didn't fully comprehend what a final act meant, but she was excited nevertheless. Then they began, silently lumbering through the village streets. Derek guided the wagon into a secluded alley and came to a halt. I must do this first, he thought. He entered the Royal Library, where the Royal Librarian was stationed behind the counter. She immediately sensed something was wrong, seeing him dressed finely in the attire of the Irindor School of Scholars. His hood was tied behind his shoulders, a position reserved for official ceremonies only.

Derek handed the book over, containing the newly added journal. Judy gazed at the drafted legacy of secrets and inventions.

"Wow!" Judy remarked. Derek, full of resolve, then hugged her in a way that conveyed a message, I may not see you again. Librarian Judy was wise, she pledged, "Derek, don't worry. I will ensure the legacy of King Richard and the Stephador Clan will be told."

However, there was also a catch that day; a spy in the shadows, a man with ill intentions, was browsing the dusty books. He was one of the many informers Quiller had placed amongst the realm. The conversation he overheard was enough to spark his interest and would have a big impact on the Second Ruby War. Yes, the journal was shared amongst Gemotroplis' four nations, but not as planned. Haley's blueprints were stolen that day, and the secrets of HAVOC were sent to Quiller.

Derek quickly returned to his wagon. As Librarian Judy realised an impending showdown was approaching, she placed the book under the counter, thinking it was safe, whilst she watched from the safety of the library window. The market square was silent as Haley approached the grand palace doors, leading a small crowd of women and children. Her steps were cautious on the cold, stone pavers. Unknown to her, a trap was set, and she was also being watched. Suddenly, two palace guards jumped out from behind the two black obsidian statues, swift and silent, grabbing Haley's arms with a vice-like grip. The women and children scattered to the back of the market square. Their attempt to flee was in vain, as they too were quickly encircled by palace guards, who pointed spears. They were all now forced to witness the upcoming events.

"Let go of me!" Haley's defiant shout rang out. The noise drew Richard's attention, and he raced over to Haley. With his Topaz cloak fluttering, he drew his sword. Emperor Maroon then stepped through the palace doors, an ominous sign that he was ready for a fight.

"Let go of her!" Richard ordered. The clan's grand plan was crumbling even before they reached the palace stairs. Out of nowhere, a mysterious yellow light flashed over Haley. In an instant, the guards staggered back, releasing their hold on her. Richard froze, his eyes widening in disbelief as the yellow light coalesced into an ethereal glow surrounding Haley. Time seemed to slow.

As the glow faded, Haley stood still, her shape now like solid stone—a stunning sculpture, a statue fit for Peroa herself. A gasp escaped Richard's lips, and his sword fell to the ground. Panic and despair marred his face as he reached out to touch Haley, searching for any sign of life.

"What have you done?" Richard's voice trembled with a mixture of anger and grief. Walking past the two obsidian statues, Maroon was in full battle dress and a red robe. He appeared as a sinister silhouette against the palace's crimson wavire backdrop. The Ruby emperor held a glowing jewel that radiated an otherworldly aura, its brilliance casting an eerie glow on his menacing features. Richard had never seen anything like it before.

"What sort of trickery is this? That was a Topaz spell! That's impossible!" Richard bellowed.

"You would think so!" Maroon smirked. "A statue of the goddess Peroa will look good in my chamber." Maroon's cold laughter echoed through the air as he revelled in the chaos he had wrought. "Foolish Topaz scum," he sneered. "You dare to rebel against the Ruby Nation. You're so predictable."

Richard clenched his fists, his anger obvious. "Undo this, release her!"

Maroon's sinister grin widened. "Release her, you are a foolish boy! I thought you would be educated in Topaz magic. That spell is one of many that can't be undone. A permanent transfiguration has no cure. Ask your father, Autumn. Oh, wait, that's impossible, isn't it, young Richard Rallian? It turns out you're much dumber than I thought." Maroon venomously cackled. The glow from Maroon's jewel started to pulse, casting more ominous light that appeared to dance before his eyes. Richard, caught between desperation and fury, considered his next move.

"But... It can't be," stuttered Richard

Unexpectedly, Maroon then tucked the jewel away in his robe and offered an act of mercy. "How about we settle this properly?" said Maroon as he drew an old sword from his sheath. The blade was chipped and rusted, the gold handle tarnished and dull. He smirked at Richard, a sinister glint in his eyes. "Recognise this blade, Richard?" Maroon's voice dripped with malice. "This is BlunderBee, the weapon my father, Cranium, swung in the first Ruby War."

Undeterred, Richard picked up his sword from the ground, Dazzldern, its poisoned metal gleaming in the sunlight. "Recognise this blade, Maroon?" Richard returned. "It's the sword that the Emperor Irindor used to defeat your father in the same war." There was a brief moment of stand-off, as the two stared intensely into each other's eyes.

"These blades haven't crossed for over fifty rots," Richard declared, his gaze locked onto Maroon. Then the two rushed towards each other. With a clash of steel, they engaged in a fierce swordfight, each strike echoing with the weight of history. The rust on the BlunderBee blade meant sparks flew with every hit. However, Richard soon realised he couldn't match Maroon's skill in a straight swordfight. Maroon parried Richard's blade with a quick manoeuvre, causing it to slip from his grasp. Panic set in as Richard scrambled to recover his weapon.

Maroon advanced, a cold smile on his lips, confident in his impending victory. But Richard, undeterred, seized the opportunity for an unexpected move. With a quick roll, he retrieved his sword and drove Dazzldern into a crack on the stone pedestal where Maroon's statue once stood. The blade sank in, securing itself. Richard was surprised by how easily it slid into the stone, like pushing a knife into butter.

Maroon's eyes widened in disbelief and even a speck of confusion. "What the hell are you doing?"

"I am done fighting." Richard declared, as he stood, rolling the Sapphire lighter with his thumb and lighting up his last cigar. Then there was silence. Maroon re-sheathed BlunderBee, taunting, "Scared? Huh?" Richard didn't respond, but just blew smoke into the emperor's face. Richard just stood there, resolute as a rock, facing the emperor who had been the root of his troubles from the very beginning — from the death of his father, to the tragic death of his mother, the loss of his brother, and even just now, the loss of Haley.

From a side alley, Derek appeared, pulling the wagon. He was dressed impeccably in his robe of the Irindor School of Scholars. He pulled up directly behind Richard. The heavy blanket Judy had given Richard was now draped over the top of the wagon, hiding the cargo inside.

Maroon stood amused at the sight, as he again reached for the *Heart of Gemotronia*. Richard turned to face the crowd, cigar in hand. "People of Royal Village," he began, his words cutting through the air. "Today, we stand here before the emperor. I may not be a leader, but I am somebody who has led in the pursuit of justice."

Maroon just laughed…

A voice echoed from the back of the square, behind the women and children surrounded by guards. "We will remember King Richard Rallian." The Royal Librarian, Judy, held tightly onto the book 'The Ruby Palace,' unaware that it was now missing the important blueprints.

He kept going, "I've hijacked an armoured transport cart! I've raided the ruby palace stores, stolen the Royal Treasury, and burnt every statue and symbol of the emperor. Now I'm here, in front of the emperor himself!"

The emperor frustratedly added, "And ruined my breakfast!"

With a confident voice, Richard then turned and addressed the emperor. "This, Maroon, is the Royal Ruby Treasury. I wanted you to witness the spoils of war. We return them now to you." His words hung in the air, brimming with defiance. The Emperor licked his lips at those words.

"Yes, every last ruby," gleamed a satisfied Maroon. Richard's eyes burned with intensity. "Remember this day, my friends," he declared, "for it is the day we sparked a change, a change that will reclaim our future from the ashes of the past." Richard's voice rang out in a very ominous tone as he voiced his final words. He turned to face Maroon once again, staring death in his eyes.

"You know, manes are born from fire!"

With those words, he signalled Derek, who swiftly removed the oil-soaked blanket covering the wagon, revealing the large open barrel filled to the brim with crimson oil. Unsurprisingly, there were no rubies. The moment was tense, the onlookers frozen in anticipation. "What is this? Where are my rubies?" Maroon bellowed.

With a solemn smile, Richard added, "They also die from fire. It's been fun. Bye, Maroon!" With one last drag, he took the cigar from his mouth and flung it over his head. The cigar, a final spark of defiance, fell onto the blanket, and the crimson oil burst into flame.

BOOM

The large barrel detonated, engulfing Richard in a wall of flames. Richard and Derek were instantly reduced to ash. The blast caught the emperor off guard. He was thrown, landing ten yards back, a painful thud against the palace doors. The heat was so intense that the sword Dazzldern was forever fused into the stone pedestal. Although the throng of villagers and the guards were some distance away, they could still feel the scorching heat on their faces and fled.

Surprisingly, the emperor, although battered and scorched, survived the ordeal. He only sustained minor injuries and burns; his robe was singed, but somehow he managed to escape alive. He was protected by the jewel in his hand, the Heart of Gemotronia.

"Ahh, my head." The emperor was dazed, staggering back to his feet. "Those little Topaz reatrits." He spat. "Quiller…" he screamed.

Maroon then reached for the other blade at his side, different from BlunderBee. As he unsheathed it, he proclaimed, "Here she is." Staring at the gleaming steel, he continued, "It's time for a new chapter. You will taste rivers of Topaz blood." He held high, his newest blade, Irisavire, as a symbol of Ruby Nation's new beginning.

Quiller, hearing his emperor's call, now stood at the scorched palace doors, surveying the destruction. Maroon yelled again at his closest advisor, his voice echoing through Royal Ruby Town.

"Quiller, this truly marks the start of the new war. Remind our mate, Colonel Manor, that the tournament in Bandeira must get underway. I need a new Realm Marshal!"

End of the Tale – Rubies & Rivals

Glossary

Acerbo-ironia: a brewed acid that can melt through almost anything. It must be stored in a glass jar or bottle, is not for drinking, and is dangerous to carry.

Archna-stela pelsitch-avia-bonwax-aroasiza: powerful, good magic, the bright light of Peroa, a spell from the mother of life.

Arachna-vire: a gemotro known as the *'Arac-vire'* or locally named *'Wendy'*. She is the mother wavire; cursed by Peroa, she retreated to her cave in the Banderian mountains.

aztel fern: a troublesome weed from the Emerald Forest; the only positive aspect is that they are edible and taste like muddy cabbage. A green fern with spikey leaves; see Bandeira nettle. In small amounts, it is used as a herb.

Bandeira nettle: the name for aztel fern in Bandeira; it's a vexing botanical pest across Gemotronia. In the verdant realms of Azareni, the Emerald folk have aptly dubbed it the *'azareni devil'*. It has spread across the hunting grounds of Bandeira, the Crimson Forest and the Jackale. Other names include Bandeira bush weed.

bellowers: ghost-like figures wearing dark cloaks; first discovered in rot: 244 era: 2nd. Gemotros that transform to lure victims. Folk tales are told to scare children in the Irindorian village so as not to wander off alone.

Bifurcation spell: a forbidden Ruby spell to cut a man in half; dark magic.

blood orchid: a flower also known as crimson bloom, found in the Crimson Forest. Its pollen dust is flammable and glows bright blue when burnt. It runs some lanterns for a much brighter light. It's also a disinfectant when crushed.

Blood Orchid (the sword): a blade gifted by Emperor Maroon to the Realm Marshal of the Ruby Army, a curved version of Irisavire.

BlunderBee: blade of Emperor Cranium wielded in the first Ruby War, crafted long ago by the blacksmiths of Gorlith. The blade was passed to Emperor Maroon.

bracklia: a gemotro that inhabits Ravena, a most dangerous grombler thought to be extinct. Its body resembled a monstrous magical amalgamation of molten basalt and flesh, its thick, armoured hide undulating like flowing lava.

butter orchid: a flower, see golden devtark.

cobbler: a special grombler, much larger and more muscular than other gromblers; they use massive wooden clubs and can throw mountain boulders to start avalanches.

colaies: the birds of Gemotroplis, created with a song by Peroa.

Chapidodia: a giant female hexapus; a gemotro that inhabited the waters off the coast of Topaz Nation from rot: 330 era: 1st to rot: 2 era: 4th. After her death, she lay on the Beach of Neil. Some folks would say '*For the rest of her time and ours*'.

crimson berries: the fruit used to brew crimson cider, and are a secret ingredient for enhanced crimson oil.

crimson cider: a delectable elixir with origins in the early days of the realm, when rot: 34, era: 1st witnessed the discovery of Crimson Berries within the heart of the Crimson Forest, by Sapphire traveller, Zeldil Haratchi, he covertly absconded with the cherished recipe.

Crimson Forest: the largest forest that dominates Ruby Nation, a forest of crimson trees.

crimson oil: the precious oil derived from the sap of the crimson tree; when impurities are removed, it becomes highly flammable. When enhanced, it's the most destructive substance in Gemotroplis, better than magic.

Daradero: cold-hearted male god of death and war.

Dazzldern: a famous sword that the Topaz Emperor Irindor wielded during the Ferinthor cavalry charge during the first Ruby War, defeating Emperor Cranium. Also wielded by Richard Rallian against Emperor Maroon. The famous sword was forged by the IronShard family.

elder maroon: a fake ruby, like fool's gold. The word *'elder'* means fake. Ironically, the name of the Ruby Emperor is also Maroon.

Emede Vinato: Emerald spell; Emedella green vines shooting from the ground, entangling and trapping your victim.

Emerald Mallet: named *'Gorungun Hengi'*, it unfolds as a remarkable testament to its power and enigmatic nature. This battle hammer bears an origin deeply intertwined with the annals of Gemotroplis.

egunis: also named a thornfish, is a Ruby gemotro, similar to a small plesiosaur with a barracudina head.

era: a timescale used in Gemotroplis; indicating each eruption of the volcano in Ravena; indicating a thousand rots - rotations; each rot similar to a year.

Fazz Fire: a teleportation potion only reserved for the Ruby Army. An alternative to the Gone Gazz.

ferinthor: large horses from the fields of Gondor in the Topaz Nation, gemotro with a mane of fire that scares off predators when threatened; used as cavalry.

fluro flutters: flowers of the Sapphire Nation used to preserve meats, better than salt, although with a minty taste; a Gemotroplis trading commodity.

Gamber Goth-Gorian: a knock-down Ruby spell, a small ball of magic fire that is more force than burn.

Gemotro: a unique creature, a non-human, given life by Peroa, the goddess of life.

Gemotronia: goddess of magic, the jealous sister of Peroa and Daradero. Her heart was shattered into eight shards, the basis of all nations' magic. She is also known as Queen Gemotronia.

golden devtark: Nicknamed butter orchid, it can be mistaken for a Topaz blossom. It's prized as it's used to brew the potion Gone Gazz and is an ingredient in a bandeiran bush weed poison. First discovered in rot: 51 era: 1st by King Jackale.

Gone Gazz: teleportation potion only reserved for the Ruby Army. An alternative to the orange powder is known as Fazz Fire.

Grutoterian: the native language of the Emerald Nation.

Hella-scaren-peta-shingo: Topaz spell; a summoned firestorm.

herpeta-mosa: nicknamed jabber, a large water-dwelling carnivore, species mosa-gac-lagas, similar to a crocodile. The first species of gemotro, emerged rot: 0 era: 1st.

Irisavire: sword of Emperor Maroon.

jabber: see herpeta-mosa.

King Richard's Wine: Richard's Wine, often dubbed the *'Invisibility shot'*, is a truly extraordinary elixir with the remarkable ability to make anybody invisible.

Loomapa-lingera: powerful topaz magic used to turn your enemy to stone.

manes: see stephador.

Muzzle Mud: a potent dark blue potion, an elixir that heals wounds, knits fractured bones, wards off ailments, and even dispels intoxication and mental turmoil. Ineffective against infection.

muzzle-myers: or the root walkers, are herbivores that are critically endangered. Inhabit the Crimson Forest and Dalenia in the northern Areden Forest. First emerged rot: 1 era: 1st. Peroa spawned these tree-like humanoids. Myer blood is the main ingredient for the Muzzle Mud potion.

Obsidian Axe: during rot: 201 era: 1st, the Obsidian Axe was born, crafted from a colossal chunk of obsidian discovered deep within the mines. Its true power, however, was unveiled by Verneto Havata, empowering it to shatter the mythical demotrite, including the revered sword of Daradero.

octave: a timescale used in Gemotroplis; a 12-day week; five octaves per quintet.

Olde Hickory: A merchant from Crimson Village, a timber cutter who wanted to tame the Great Ruby River. He built a lock, dam and stone bridge during the late era: 2nd, all of which still stand.

Ornithialk: a giant eagle-like creature created in rot: 60 era: 1st by Peroa. Some say she remains nesting in the Bandeiran mountains.

Paxta-holla: Ruby spell; basic ruby fire-starting that replaces a flint & steel.

Paralapse: a forbidden Ruby spell to age your victim; dark magic.

pelata: or breed Pelor is a non-hostile herbivore whose diet consists of Banderian Bush weeds. It is an endangered species, basically a very large centipede. Pelatas were first discovered rot: 34 era: 1st in the early settlements in Galarie; early Bandeira.

Peroa: goddess of life, created all living things on Gemotroplis. A mother with the looks of a beautiful golden-haired lady.

quintet: timescale used in Gemotroplis; a month of 60 days; eight quintets per rot. Each nation refers to a quintet in its own customary way.

Ravena: .

Redemptias: a formidable Topaz gemotro akin to a gigantic gecko, indigenous to the treacherous waters of the Neilan Sea.

reatrits: giant rat-like gemotros that exist in all nations and can enter plague proportions. Also used as a derogatory term, being obscene to someone.

Re-tentro-mjana: Ruby spell; immobilising stun, can cause short-term paralysis, a guard's favourite.

rot: timescale used in Gemotroplis; a calendar year, a rot is 480-days.

sacro selester: Emerald gemotro, first emerged rot: 313 era 3rd, giant tame flying serpents similar to its ferocious cousins the sacro slither.

sacro slither: a flying serpent carnivore, an Emerald gemotro; the population is thriving, first emerged rot: 78 era 1st.

savanta: large, winged horses from the fields of Gorlith, a Sapphire gemotro. Savanta feathers were poached and harvested to produce the Muzzle Mud.

stephador: a very large gemotro akin to a tiger but the size of a hippopotamus. They hunt in packs and are aggressive. These beings originate from the forests of Areden and are locally referred to as manes.

sphyraena: locally named bloaters, omnivores (seagrass and plankton). Very large and similar to a blue whale, but not a mammal, it has four fins on its body.

saxumiaturpis: locally named boulder shark is a Topaz gemotro, a large hostile carnivore with razor teeth and a muscular tail. Imagine a tiger shark crossed with a humpback whale.

SluckStick: a machete-type blade of questionable quality.

starlight echoes: a flower thought extinct in rot: 20 era: 2nd. During the Battle of Emiella, soldiers would use the flowers for food to numb their wounds.

Sword of Daradero: the blade created by Daradero to assassinate Queen Gemotronia, the goddess.

Tipsy Tonic: a potion thrown on the ground that produces gas; when inhaled, it makes you drunker than a sailor.

turtur anguilla: Topaz gemotro, a large sea turtle about the size of a small whale.

terrortor: nicknamed Blue Blur, is a flying Sapphire gemotro like a medium-sized dragon; an omnivore.

Trio-Septeria: known as *'Fangs'*, is a mystical three-headed tiger guardian who dwells within the sacred precincts of the Temple of Gemotronia. Daradero guided Peroa herself to bestow life upon this enigmatic creature rot: 1 era: 1st.

stalker: nicknamed watcher, these hostile humanoids dwell in the Obsidian Forest. The population is estimated to be a few hundred. They bite with their teeth and claw with long fingernails; they only eat meat. First emerged rot 20: era 1st.

watcher: see a stalker.

wavire: a beastly gigantic Ruby gemotro spider. King Finch, a Ruby king, thought these creatures symbolised the Ruby Nation, as they were fierce and terrifying and were growing rapidly in population.

Wav-va-wire stella lo-compo: part of a secret recipe for disinfectant, wavire juice; not the best drink.

Wezdorth Dazzagar: Ruby spell; lightning bolts used by Ruby guards.